Dedicated to my family,
You made this all possible!

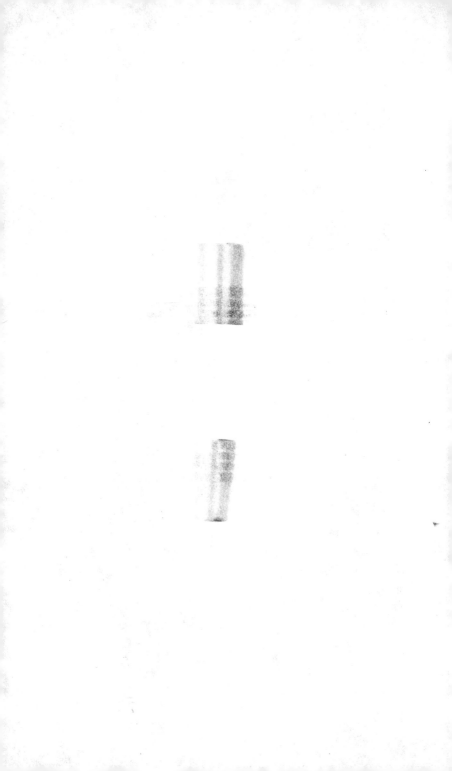

Status: At war
Climate: -40/+R
Biodiversity: 78%
Terrain: Extreme
Humanoid lifeforms: CANNOT PROCESS
Language: CANNOT PROCESS
Technology level: CANNOT PROCESS

"ERROR"   "ERROR"

"ERROR"

No Man's Land

Blizzardian Pole Border

Eastern Kelrian Border

Permaspat coast

Southern Pacific

Southern Glacier Peninsula

The Frostbjel Coast

Western Pacific

Drive computer (Cass): I'm not so sure
you'll survive long,
seeing as you never took
your training courses.

Profile: Captain Gianana
Username: Vogelkampfgeist
Password: **********

Blizzardia Region map on Jensen's PC

JENSEN

My name is Jensen Galantis. I'm probably the worst person to tell a life story, *mostly because it's only at the very end that I see the light in it all. I was born an outsider, and the world pushed its motives and agendas on my weaknesses.*

For some odd reason I was always followed around by a family member, watching me like a hawk, as if I even breathed wrong they would send me for some form of treatment.

By the time I was thirteen, I was five foot eleven and had a bad reputation for falling asleep in class. My earliest years were filled with detention and sleepless nights. Later in my childhood it only got worse, from trying to fail tests to getting poked and prodded by every psychiatrist imaginable.

Thousands of light years away from any family member at age nineteen, I didn't have the brightest opinion of life. I'm sure the last few years would have gone a lot smoother if I hadn't gotten in a fight with every brat space-brain jerk beyond Earth's atmosphere, and let my cadets get to me every time they played a practical joke. They were only thirteen, after all.

All of my life's problems seemed to start with the things I loved most. My father and my brother dying about a year and a half apart—my older brother was crushed under a pile of rocks on a space expedition when he was fourteen, and my father's death was classified as a "biological anomaly"—and my mother getting a job at Headquarters as HR Commander only made matters worse as far as my attitude went.

My family were one of the few who got to work for Cacadin, even though we're all Terrans—Earth-borns. Considering the fact that my father was fresh from the Netherlands, which would usually mean we weren't eligible for space travel within Canada for another two generations, we were lucky to get in at all. But my dad was a mental marvel when it came to all things strategy, captainship, and biological fabrication, which made it nearly impossible for Cacadin to resist.

My parents lived vicariously through me, their last living son, which meant that Biology technically wasn't my choice, and captainship wasn't, either. I sort of had to just go with it, seeing as I'd already been torn from my home planet, my friends, my school, and everything else I loved about British Columbia.

Cacadin is a space expedition colony that has probably discovered more lifeforms in fifty years than Earth has in over two hundred. They aren't the biggest company in the universe, but they are the monopoly for anyone who wants to have something to do with space, and most of the time the key to Canada's stable economy.

Cacadin Head is opposite of the sun compared to Earth, they just put a portal on each end so you can go subatomic through the sun's core. Stratum One is pinpointed in orbit inside the Kuiper Belt, Stratum Two is past the Kuiper Belt by planet Sultra, which was colonized for extra space and also where I was trained for captainship. And, last but not least, Stratum Three is literally in the middle of nowhere, a solar dead zone created by a dying star.

PROLOGUE

"Luggage pick up in: five minutes." I glared up from my carry on at a flashing red holographic sign: 5 min. Pick up. Which made me chew my aspartame-free mint gum harder.

The people clustered around the rotating track that brought luggage down from the ship where mostly high school students or Chinese tourists taking pictures of everything and everyone. There was a group of grade eleven students and a tourist group beside each other, and though they seemed to stay to their own conversations and keep their gazes from crossing, there was the odd time where you saw a tourist take a quick picture of a captain passing. Or literally anybody in a bodysuit.

My gaze turned to the glass wall behind the clusters of visitors. A ship was coming into port slowly. I squinted to see the name engraved and painted in metallic black on the side: The *Decagon*.

That was the first ever ship to have electromagnet technology. The *Decagon*, piloted by captain Calix Novak, was a multi-powered, naval class ship that was propelled by an electromagnet motor and secondary power cells that constantly re-charged to power the electric thrusters.

It was the first step to a much bigger future.

The cockpit came into view.

Novak's eyes caught me sitting on a bench and he swiveled suddenly, mouth rapidly opening and closing as he spoke to someone on the double-leveled bridge.

"Jensen Galantis, is that you?" came a voice through speakers located on the walls in the luggage pickup alcove.

I scowled as the eyes of tourists and students turned to me.

Zenon proceeded to poke me in the shoulder, even after I didn't answer the captain, and had tried—redhead, blue eyes and all—to blend in as much as possible.

"What, Zenon?" I barked as I glared at the seventeen-year-old with hazel-coloured hair, his finger seizing back mid-poke as if he were only three years old.

"C'mon Jensen, there must be some way you find joy in being noticed like that." He nodded to the ship outside as the underbelly bridge disappeared below.

Visitors were only allowed on this level as passenger yachts carried them in and out and brought them their luggage. Otherwise they were located in the secondary dome where things were more. . . normal. Here, there was another level with walking paths branching off to supply rooms and docking bays, a level with temporary offices, and finally another with sleeping quarters.

I pulled the hood of my sweater closer around my head and stuffed my hands back into the thigh-long pockets on my camo track pants. "Zenon, like I've said fifty times already, I hate. . ." my words trailed off as my attention was pulled to something in my peripheral vision. When I craned my neck to look, I found a blond-haired girl. Her long braid, thick and smooth, ended just above her waist. Her face was an elegant oval shape, with freckles on her nose and cheeks. My heart rose in my throat as the girl slowly brushed some long silvery blond hair away from her face, and paced away towards the combat gym.

I'd expect her to look lost in all the commotion, like a kid who'd lost their way to the science room at high school.

That wasn't the case at all.

In fact, to my eyes, she seemed to be more with it than any other virtuoso in this confusing reality.

"You like her! Ha, I've seen that look too many times!" Zenon joked, resting his arm on my shoulder with all his weight. Like any other computer geek, he talked in all the wrong places, watched romance movies, and still knew jack squat about love.

I looked him dead in the eyes with my icy scowl and he immediately backed off, returning his gaze to his computer. Even though I was a year younger than him, I was still taller, making everyone assume I was older.

What was I now? I remember Mother saying something about my being almost a foot taller than her, which meant I was about six foot four.

Zenon spoke in his deafening, crackling, unintentionally high-pitched voice, "Why don't you follow her?" Still staring at the glass screen of the computer he pushed his glasses up on his face.

"What? Right now? She just headed into the most dangerous part of th—"

"So? If you like her, then go and get punched in the face once or twice. With your attitude, it shouldn't be a problem," he needled, finally gazing up with his challenging seaweed-green eyes. I opened my mouth to protest when I realized he was right for once.

I let out a loud frustrated grunt before slapping my bag on the hard seat and heading towards the combat gym's large glass doors.

As I walked, getting glances and whispers from the rushing people around me, I realized how different this world had become. It hadn't grown to accept the differences of others. My gangly body structure, poker straight posture, deep blue eyes, and weird height were all the more frustrating in these situations.

Most of the women who rushed around me were quite a bit shorter, all about the average height of five six.

Not that girl.

She was different.

She had to be five nine.

That's why I was chasing her, we had something in common. . .

That and her looks of course.

I peered through the thick glass doors into the white space, then realized what I was doing and stopped myself for a brief second. *Why do I listen to anything Zenon says? He knows nothing.* Despite this, I realized that you needed a card—or something along those lines—to get in. With perfect timing, a burly, black-haired kid pushed past and used a small prism on his wristband to open the doors. I snuck in behind the shorter teenager just as the door closed behind me. He headed towards a booth that had everything from karambits and wrist braces to xiphos swords and acids. Oh, there were also pistols and guns. Don't forget that.

This three-story tall hall was about three-and-a-half high school football fields long and two wide. Large cylinder magnets on the floor retracted to the same gender on the ceiling, both hardly noticeable. I mean, I could probably trip over it, but it wasn't like a big pillar or anything. It might be an inch or two tall on both the ceiling and the floor.

There were bench presses on the end to my right, along with free weights, ellipticals, and abdominal crunchers. Parkour climbing walls curled from floor to ceiling and around in rigid effects. There were also vaulting, parallel bars, and still rings on the back wall and part of the left side.

Then, on the rest of the left wall was gun combat, a boxing division, and all the specialty stuff.

I heard the pop of a gunshot, and from the corner of my eye I saw something pointing a gun at me. I ducked as a pellet just missed me and hit one of the lockers, then whipped around to see it was a droid who had fired. I assumed it was malfunctioning. It walked towards me slowly, taking its gun in both hands as it retracted back into the loaded position.

It focused on me with a blank, automated gaze.

"Uhh . . . I'm not training." I tried to move away from the drone, and knocked over an empty garbage can. "Your students are over there," I pointed to one of the agile teenagers on the other side of the room.

I was anything but agile.

The droid's gaze was stuck to me as the bar read "level five training exercise in progress." I jerked to the side as it tried to punch me in the stomach and it ended up smashing its metal hand into one of the lockers. I turned back to face it just as it was lining up to fire again with its pellet gun.

I exchanged a worried glance with the teenager beside me, then yanked his gun out of his hands. "Hey!" he blurted.

I pulled the trigger on the long pellet gun, trying to shoot the glossy black droid. My aim was slightly off and I struck a droid on the other side of the large space, hitting its actuator in its head.

It kicked the girl it had been training, making her keel over onto her back on the floor.

"Oops. Umm . . . could I have one second to figure this thing out? Urr, pause session?" My voice cracked as the droid kept its cold, lifeless stare on me, pushing me towards the back of the gym. Its sign suddenly changed to read "fist combat in process" instead.

It was messed up alright.

"Oh, this is going to end really bad," I let out a nervous chuckle as it threw an uppercut at me, barely missing my chin. I ducked as it tried to punch me in the stomach, but forgot about its other fist just as it came around to hook me in the nose.

I let out a wail as I dropped the gun and clutched my broken, bleeding nose. Staggering back, I tried to regain my balance as the humanoid robot came at me.

"Jensen, watch out!" the blond-haired girl shouted. I looked up from my bloody hands to see the robot fall to the ground. She landed on top of it, stabbing her short sword vertically through the top of the droid.

I lurched back, startled, still staring down at the twitching robot as sparks flew.

My heart was starting to settle when she spoke in her silky, commanding tone, "Don't let this happen again, Jensen."

My heart sped up again.

"How do you know my name?" I asked, shocked. She didn't answer, just turned and walked towards the door.

CHAPTER 1

Six years later...

Why are these suits
So tight!?

Jensen Galantis

Captain Jensen Galantis (desaturated image)

I was holding a cup of black coffee, gazing down at a piece of paper with a pen held awkwardly in my mouth, when the door to the coffee room slid open.

I had noticed the movement from the corner of my eye, but didn't hear the usual hissing of the electromagnets in the shaft pumping up and down because of the earpieces drowning out every sound that surrounded me.

I kept tracing the blueprints layed out all over the table, seeing even the tiniest flaws that still existed throughout the four years I'd had this ship.

Circling one of the electromagnets on the inside edge of the motor, I wrote a note: *constant sputter cause, adjust voltage and convert battery cell three to draw power from piston.*

My music cut out as it recognized a voice.

"Hey Jensen, can . . . you. Please. Help me with these?" a tall woman asked, struggling to hold the boxes and the door simultaneously. One of the white steel cases almost slipped out of her grasp and she caught it with her knee.

She grunted and messed with her bottom lip as her concentration was almost broken by my swiveling to snag her gaze.

"Sure," I answered tiredly as I stood up from the table, causing the hover chair to slide across the room. It hit the long island, which held a coffee machine and a few plants to add decoration to the quartz counter and white walls.

I tried to rub away the sleep in my eyes gently with my pointer finger as I stepped stiffly towards her.

She took in my face for a few moments with a worried expression. I wasn't sure if it was the wiry stubble, the bags under my eyes, or the cuts on my cheek bones, jaw, forehead, and eyebrows.

"You look like you haven't slept in days." She handed me a few of the boxes, stretching out her strained muscles. I thought she was maybe trying to ignore everything else that was going on with my face. "Oh, last night was your night shift, right? How was it?"

2

"Ugh! Trust me, Tesla, you don't want to know," I warned, slapping my ear with the palm of my hand to try and turn off the music that pounded my eardrums. My sound-blocking earbuds were the only thing that seemed to soothe the agony of being a captain twenty-four seven. When it came to Tesla, though, even her voice seemed to help me cope.

I had a sudden recollection of the horrible night I'd had.

Cacadin Stratum Three was the farthest spaceport from Earth and was the last stop before we got to Annoterra. The pilots of ships from Cacadin already had enough on their plates, but Cacadin Head command thought that, on top of everything else their teams had to deal with, they would shove another task in our faces: loading our own export luggage.

Cacadin would regret it this time, seeing as they lost more than five captains last year due to the permanent closing of all spaceship mechanics in the system.

I, of course, was against this and complained to them at the meeting, since the people who usually handle our goods are professionals.

To make things more complicated, on Xomnia, the last place my crew and I had been, we picked up these horrific plants with a really fancy scientific name. I just called them tarragon plants because they reminded me of the herb I always found revolting. But hey, it was better than getting samples from stars.

Or that's what I thought before the unexpected happened.

Last night after the meeting, I opened the entrance to the export bay and suddenly was chucked across the large space by a massive vine.

I landed on shards of glass that were lying haphazardly on the floor. I winced to see my hands and face were cut and bleeding and a small piece stabbed deep into my thigh, but other than that nothing was badly damaged.

I was a little dizzy as I attempted to stand, and was swept back off my feet onto the floor. This time I let out a small wheeze as I tried to get up. My vision cleared to reveal a blue-red serpent-like plant. It fixed its attention on one of the captains who had come to claim some of his resources.

The only reason he was here was because he needed replacement parts for his ship, *Seriatim*. Unlike a heavy duty machine, spaceships are fragile, and require new hoses and such if you are puttering along on the outer reaches. They should have fared much better, though, even with keeping up on maintenance. And it's not like these parts were cheap, either. One custom stock fitting cost around two thousand units. I would go broke yet if I didn't do something properly for once, and I knew it.

Well, I've dealt with worse, I thought, trying to make out the captain through my near-sighted eyes. When I realized who it was, I was immediately concerned.

The captain did not listen well and tended to be very obnoxious.

"Captain Magnus! You need to let me take care of that plant!" I shouted across the large space, trying to catch the man's attention.

"I don't want your help!" he said as he tried to shoot the swift plant and ended up shooting a mercury light. We glanced at each other in a you're-dead sort of way, realizing what he had just done. He was suddenly, casually tossed across the room as if the plant was bored. He smacked into the solid wall with his back, then fell to the ground lifelessly as he blacked out. I held back a small chuckle at the comic timing, replying with a hardly convincing "sorry" shouted across the room.

My true emotions spilled out and I rolled my eyes, blasting the oversized venus fly trap quickly in the back of the head. *I gave Magnus his chance to kill it, leave it up to the master biologist to do it properly.* I scooted around the mercury spill to the unconscious captain as the tarragon plant fell to the ground with a huge, earthquake-like thud.

I snapped back into reality and noticed I was gazing at Tesla blankly. She gave me a weird look and I blinked multiple times forcefully, turning my gaze back to the box to avoid the awkwardness. I could feel my palms start to sweat. I'd made myself look like an idiot for what seemed like the millionth time this week. I'd fallen down the stairs to the sleeping quarters yesterday, attempting to ask Tesla out for coffee while we were still at Stratum Three. Instead of a date, the result was a bleeding nose and lip and fractured confidence.

I read the writing engraved into the top of the box: *Coffee Room/Breakfast.* I wanted to rip open the case and examine its contents, but knowing I wouldn't get to eat any of the delicious consumables for another three hours due to my detoxification medication, all I could do was let nausea pound on my head and my stomach tighten and growl.

Stupid tarragon plant.

Stupid air canister seals.

That's why I needed the detox meds. The air on Xomnia was toxic and, if you breathed it in, it would cause your blood toxicity to spike.

But the plants couldn't live without it, so we needed to bottle it up and send calibrations and research back to Headquarters so they could fabricate more.

Xomnia was, by far, the planet with the most dangerous forests in the entire galaxy, full of tarragon plants with fangs as big as a human arm. We needed a few of the tarragon plants for the greenhouse, and as part of the training exercises for our missions.

My cadets thought they were somehow created on Earth years ago and relocated to Xomnia so they wouldn't hurt anybody.

Did I believe this?

Yes. No. Maybe so.

Annoterra was also full of ravenous animals. Luckily we were being sent to a snowy place, a region called Blizzardia, where, technically, the only thing that can kill a human within twenty-four hours is either extreme cold or avalanches.

The bitter, frayed ends of Canada, as I called it.

"So, in that case, not the best night shift," Tesla snickered, blowing some of her long blond hair out of her face as it fell out of the braid.

"Give me a break," I growled under my breath. "I think a better example, Tesla, is my painful experience being thrown into the atomic gate as a prank from our wonderful cadets." I resisted snapping at her, knowing I could regret it.

I remembered the prank's details very clearly: Get Captain Jensen to the portal bridge, tell him there was a woman stuck on the backside of the gate. Captain Jensen goes out there, and we deactivate his gear, sending him into the atomic gate.

They'd been planning it for days.

But I guess that's what I get for training a bunch of teenagers. At the time they were thirteen and the naughtiest kids in the world.

Back then, I was a tempermental nineteen-year-old.

"I was not a part of that," she defended, tightening her brow as we brought the boxes over to the island in the middle of the room.

"So, how long until Annoterra?" Tesla asked, using the ship's cargo code to open the box.

I started to answer but just then a sharp vibration shook the entire ship, knocking my helmet off the glass table. I snatched it up off the polished white floor and attached it to my back as I rushed out the door and down the hallway, Tesla following close behind.

The rumble came again, but this time it hurled us both against the wall. I hit my head and wished I'd put my helmet on.

The LED lights flickered and I tried to get back onto my feet against the awkwardness of the slanted floor as the ship was pushed off course, tilted to its side slightly.

"Quick! We need to get to the control room!" I urged, grabbing her wrist and pulling her up and forward with me.

We ran as swiftly as we could to the bridge. Tesla gave me the same anxious look she did when the team wasn't paying attention.

I unlocked the door and it hissed open.

I was overwhelmed when I found the proximity alerts going off, and surprised to see everyone in their correct positions, doing what they were supposed to for once. Maybe the pressure was finally smartening them up—either that, or it was because of all those annoying practice drills.

"Captain!" My attention was pulled to a short man, his eyes wide with horror. "If they continue at this rate we will be blown to pieces in under five minutes!"

"Please calm down, Dax. I don't want to hurt anyone or give a bad impression," I answered calmly.

But really, if I were to be honest, I was thinking the same thing.

"Right, sorry Captain. Although I will still bring them online," Daxon apologized, swiping his information over to a small tablet connected to a swiveling bar at his eye level.

I strode up to my controls and squinted at the black space outside my ship. My emotions flipped like a switch when I saw the battlefield set out in front of my dreadnought, the *Annex*, making my ship seem meagre. The *Annex*'s weapons were no match for the oversized battle-ready canons of the inhabitors.

We're hooped! I thought hopelessly as my eyes searched the control board beneath my hands for any signs of hope.

"Zenon, can you get a reading on their weapons?" I looked across the room to a man leaning over a control panel.

He adjusted his new dark green glasses and answered with a worried expression, "No, I can't, the coding on these ships is impenetrable." He sat farther forward in his seat to stare at the odd coding. "If we'd known there where natives on this planet we could have—"

"I know, Zenon, just do your job." I cut him off before he could finish. I couldn't handle the pressure.

Everyone's lives on this ship were at stake. If they died or got hurt, their loss would be on my shoulders.

He didn't take his eyes off the screen, settling his fingers on the keyboard to punch in some more numbers.

"Cadet Jasper, can you maybe get a transmission through?" I asked again. The ship took another hit, on the bow this time, crinkling the glass in an array of long webs.

"It seems I don't have to, Captain, they're sending us a transmission . . . and . . . got it!"

"Captain Jensen Galantis— yes, I know who you are— if you've just come to toy with our plants and animals then leave now," the voice said forcefully.

Although I could not see him I imagined a very sinister alien.

I looked at the crew's mortified faces before taking a deep breath. "No, we are here to do research, not—" I was cut off when they unexpectedly rained fire on us. I had to throw my helmet on, the only thing that could protect me from the minus two hundred and seventy degrees Celsius outer space. *But what about the rest of the crew!?* I suddenly thought about how they did not have the same protection.

9

But before I could even look up from my steering console the bow broke, sending shattered glass everywhere, ejecting my crew into space.

I grabbed a piece of railing by the stairs down to the other consoles for dear life, though my hands got cold and started to lose their strength.

I ordered myself not to let go.

I wouldn't dare let go if it meant I would still have dignity.

My hands slipped more. *Don't you dare!* My mind gasped as the muscles in my right hand gave in, lowering it to my side.

My last hope before my left hand gave in was to try and reaffirm my jetpack, which, last time I'd tried to use it, had stopped working in mid-air and landed me in a swamp.

I tried it, though. It only sent sparks flying out of the bridge.

As I attempted to pull myself back up toward the railing, one of the bolts cracked off.

Then another.

The last one broke and I was torn from my ship—sent into the outer atmosphere of Annoterra.

I threw the piece of railing to the side and gazed around to find myself in a purple galaxy. My heart rose in my throat as I looked in the debris for the rest of my crew and failed to find any of them. Trying to move around, I found that half of my body was numb. The two moons of Annoterra were covered in a gray-blue haze. I guessed this was a result of them circling around Annoterra twice as fast: our scientists at Cacadin Headquarters had observed this occurrence every other year. *What could I expect when I bring a crew to*

an alien planet, without any information about the life forms?
The ships surrounding me created a battlefront expanse, protecting the entire area we were supposed to investigate, like a blanket of mesh.

My thoughts were quickly cut off by the excruciating pain that came from my hands as they built up with frost.

I lifted them to my face, examining the thick icicles that protruded.

After a few moments I was forced into a fitful sleep.

CHAPTER 2

I was roused by a loud shriek which instantly sent my heart racing. I vaulted to my feet, my gaze jolting any which way so I could take in the masses of dead, human-like beings. The area around me gave the impression of a smooth black box you could run on forever and get nowhere. The source of light wasn't visible from any angle, it was simply illuminating from the air, as if it were a drawing that an inexperienced artist had tried to shade.

What or who did this? I crouched down on one knee to inspect one of the pale bodies, horror written on its hexagon-marked face. The anatomy was somewhat human from what I could observe: there were two arms, two legs, a head with normal simplistic features such as a nose, ears, and eyes.

However, the rest was extraterrestrial: odd protrusions stuck out from the sides of its head, and when I poked its cheek to make the head roll to the side, I saw that the deviations carried around the back in a steep slope downwards to follow the cranium. The ears were long and rounded at the end, with the look of a deer's but the texture of something smoother than human skin, almost polished. There were markings all over the sides of the face, under the eyes, on the

13

ears, and anywhere else that was visible from beneath the unfamiliar uniform it wore.

I stood up quickly to dodge a yellow sulphur bullet, which, if it weren't for my keen sense of hearing, would have hit me in the head. I spun around, glowering as the blob turned into the figure of a pale teal extraterrestrial.

He came closer to me and I saw the gold irises of his eyes, which looked like they had been dulled by pain and other emotions over time. His brows had hardened into a scowl. The places where he had no pale, glowing squares, such as his nose, cheeks, forehead, ears, and arms—which were partly hidden under a sweater rolled up to the elbow so they wouldn't get soaked with the blood that dripped from his hands—were plastered with deep blue freckles. On top of the grey sweater he wore a leather vest with what seemed like six or seven pockets. His pants were sturdy, and although I didn't know what they were made of or why they were baggy, I could see they messed with his build completely.

My gaze jolted to the huge gun he swung back over his shoulder. He sneered as he saw the panic on my face.

Well, there's my answer!

The corrupt alien pulled and shot again, and this time as I threw myself to the side I noticed the aliens on the ground and the alien shooting at me were the same species. I reached for my gun holster only to find it wasn't there. I felt around my clothes for any type of weapon but all I found was the same old armoured shell. I got up and tried to retreat but another bullet hit me in the upper back. Why I thought that would work I don't even know, it was probably a mixture of fight or flight and the fact that I had no idea what was going on. I fell to the ground as soon as the bullet hit me, paralyzed from the shoulders down. I didn't feel the pain until just before I blacked out.

There was an automated voice far off, clouded and tinny from the ringing in my ears, "Nervous system rebooting . . . bone integrity regenerating . . ." I sucked in a sharp breath in a split second of consciousness, gasping for air while choking it back out.

Who was that? How on Earth am I still alive? I was shot out into space, and my crew . . . my thoughts trailed off. My nerves pulsed with the dull pain that the dream gave me as I tried to move. The frigid air made my cyan blue eyes itch, filling them with unwanted tears. My muscles tensed and released a few times, making me comprehend that I was securely clamped to a vertical slab of metal. Tucked under my black microfiber base layer were various cords that then snaked away to the floor, trailing out of view behind the slab. My thick hair dangled in front of my face, soaked from sweat, distorting my vision as I observed the wires closely: blue, red, and yellow.

The three primary colours? I puzzled.

"Ugh." My back hurt as I stretched as best I could, fixating on my surroundings. A blue glow illuminated an odd-looking computer box that sat beside the slab. I imagined that was where the cords went eventually, recording heart rates, brainwaves and . . . memories! *I'm going to destroy that thing as soon as I get free!* I raged, glaring at the box as if it might simply get up and attack me.

My breath stank so bad, but I couldn't help re-inhaling the same breath once in a while. Through my blurry eyes, I could see shelves filled with what looked like medicine bottles. Every object in the room had a label on it, written in odd symbols. I squinted to see more and saw a huge door on the other side of the room, which made me consider the possibility that this was a large, secluded location, considering there were no windows and the walls and ceiling appeared to be painted white metal.

I noticed my thin belt on the floor with the Cacadin Headquarters gun holster. It was folded without any crinkles . . . wait, what? How could someone possibly fold so neatly? Folding double helix DNA strands and reconfiguring cells I could do, but I was horrible at folding anything that fit under the category 'flexible'. I didn't know how Tesla, or anyone for that matter, did it so well.

Well, that's a start. As my gaze fell to the belt I also noticed that my feet were not clamped.

Why didn't they tie my feet down? I could surely reach my gun with my feet . . . and then somehow . . . escape. I let out a depressed sigh. I kind of hung there, putting all my body weight solely on my wrists. It hurt, but it was the only way to make sure I wouldn't cramp up my entire upper half, making me look like a solidified, frozen person.

I then felt a large, sharp rumble, which made some of the bottles shake on their shelves.

A ship! My heart skipped a beat as it suddenly came to me that might be my ticket out of here. Now I had a reason to get my gun. I tried to reach it with my large, knee-high boots, and with luck, passed it from my feet to my mouth. This probably looked quite dorky, as I had no way to keep my saliva from dripping onto the black box that was attached to my holster. An array of whites formed in my hand into a small gun that had a canister on it for the plasma. I closed my eyes, hoped and prayed that it would work without making too much racket. Fortunately the gun made only a small snap, and the cuffs clattered to the polished gray floor.

I put my blaster away and noticed that the floor consisted of hematite, which explained the glossy gray colour. Despite the unused feeling that lingered in the room, it had no signs of dust or grime.

I unpinned the wires from my chest and, remembering the medical machine, kicked it as hard as I could. I let out a small shout of agony as I stubbed *all* my toes on my left foot. I grabbed my injured foot in my hands and grunted angrily under my breath. I grabbed my gun and shot the machine into pieces instead. I quickly put on my black exofiber suit, the glide shell, and gun holster.

"Aww. . . yuck!" I whispered as I got my saliva all over my hand. I wiped it off quickly and grabbed my helmet, snapping it on with determination. My face was almost numb from the chill of the room, which made me realize that this was either underground or . . . what I feared . . . I was on the outskirts of the Blizzardia region. This led me to a worrying thought: *How am I going to endure and find my team without literally freezing to death? How does anybody do it? Destiny? Fate? I swear I will probably get killed before I even get into the outside world . . .* Then I abruptly had to push that disturbing thought out of my mind for, again, I felt a large rumble. There were symbols located on the right side of the sliding doors, almost glowing in contrast to the dull coloured walls and jars. I assumed it displayed 'open', so I shrugged and used my pointer finger to push the green button. It slid open quickly with an almost sizzling sound. What I saw was nothing short of the word alien: a black geometric bismuth-like corridor stood before me, making it hard to tell the difference between the walls and a corner. The smell out here was much different than in the room. It had more of a metallic odour and it was even colder. I reached out to touch one of the walls and felt a slight shock jolt my arm. I was also surprised to find that the grease did not rub off when I touched the wall. *Perhaps it's not grease after all*, I thought.

The corridors were desolate, making me wonder if the place was abandoned. *Is there any way—* my thought was cut off when I suddenly banged into a wall as the hall turned a corner to meet an oversized door.

"Huh." I was startled to see a door this big, considering there seemed to be no other hallways or doors, only pas-sageways. *There's clearly nobody here . . . maybe I could just fry the circuits and it would slide open? Seems like the only way,* I decided, concentrating my energy on the gun. It again formed in my left hand. I felt its shape, hoping that I would never lose one of the only pieces of Earth I had left. *What happens to me depends on where I am . . . either Annoterra . . . or an alien ship.* I thought. I paused, trying to find the perfect angle, and then, with one swift movement I shot the circuit, turning it to a sizzling molten mess. Again there were blue, yellow, and red wires. *That was a little more than a fry! Hah! Take that, Cacadin safety agent!* I scoffed. I was astonished to see the door crawl open with a horrible scratching noise. As it slid open a crack it let in a large amount of white natural light, which led me to realize how dark it was inside. Through the door I could see a hanger with a large ship, much like the ones that attacked me and my crew. I squeezed the gun tightly with anger. I felt that sudden rage again, but this time I didn't do anything to appease it. I pushed it away, hoping it would go elsewhere. *Why do I have so many of these feelings? I can't get upset . . . this happened . . . I can't go back and fix it. Fix what I can now.* I squeezed through the small space while the door was still in the midst of opening. To my surprise, I found a snowy, cold, mountainous world. I took in a deep breath of the fresh air when I was hit with a frightening thought. *I'm in Blizzardia . . .*

CHAPTER 3

No Man's Sky

I was so overwhelmed with that thought it took me a moment to realize the ship was lifting off the bay floor into the air. I stood staring through my tinted-glass helmet at the snowy plateau, filled with horror. The wind blew furiously, making the landscape look more like a whitecapped ocean than a snow-covered, desolate wasteland. The ship battered searing hot air at my suit and I ran straight for the vessel, adrenaline pulsing through my body. The lens on my helmet got foggy as I pelted to catch up with the ship, my gun swishing back and forth in my hand.

"I knew this would happen! First day on a strange planet. Man, snap out of it, Jensen!" I said under my breath, panting. I put my gun away in order to press a small glass pallet on the wrist of my suit, which activated a grappling hook that I aimed at the sluggishly closing cargo pad. I nearly missed as the aircraft lifted off into the sky, but managed to catch the edge of a support bar and was yanked onto the floor just as the cargo pad door closed all the way. I heaved a large breath and let out a chuckle, taking off my helmet. I brushed my fingers through my thick copper hair as I gazed into the black, smooth glass of my helmet and rubbed off the condensation. The incredibly clean glass reminded me of the many times I had to watch my father take off in his huge spaceship into the outer reaches of the galaxy, disappearing for weeks on end to who knows where.

This brought back one of my earliest memories: I was sitting next to a large window near the kitchen table, watching as the ship took off from a launch pad far to the north. The large pines outside shook, making the snow fall off into the wind. I had let out a large sigh. My mother came up to me slowly and looked out the window with her cup of morning coffee. She set her hand on my back reassuringly.

"I wish I could go on space expeditions like Father," I said, looking forlornly down at a drawing I had done. The picture had a small boy in it, shaking hands with a classic alien from a movie I had watched.

"You will, Jensen, when you're older," my mother laughed. I met her smiling brown eyes.

"Someday, when you are older, we will leave Earth and train you to be one of the best Cacadin explorers in the system!" my mother had said.

Now, I felt a tear fall from my cheek, remembering how long ago that was, and that I might never see my home planet again, or the people I loved. *This is my first mission. I've failed so miserably. Got attacked by an alien species, got trapped in a medical room, and now on an alien spaceship! That's just great!*

Ironically, my wish had come true only a few years later, when I was eleven.

I set the helmet beside me and looked about the small, dark space. Here I saw large cylinders, filled with red phosphorescent spheres. There were mysterious markings on the sides of the cylinders. *I really wish I could read this!* I thought as I looked closer, puzzled. *The language is made up of symbols . . . like splashes of mercury?* I reached out to touch them and was relieved not to be shocked again. I stood up, looking more closely at the walls and the ceiling. *No doors . . . no buttons . . .* this was a very disturbing thought.

Cacadin, what the heck is wrong with you? You said there were no carbon-based life forms on this planet! Headquarters had long-range cameras to see into the atmosphere of planets before expeditions. So you would assume they would know if a planet was inhabited or not.

Suddenly I was flung to the ceiling when the craft dropped in altitude and came to a complete stop on what I assumed was a landing pad of some sort.

"Oof!" I shouted as all the air was knocked out of my lungs and I slammed onto the floor beside one of the capsules. I reached my right hand up to my nose and wasn't surprised to find it was bleeding, but not broken.

Man, that hurt!

Annoyed by the pain, I sat up awkwardly still holding my nose, looking straight up at the ceiling to stop the bleeding.

"Ugh!" I responded to the gross feeling of blood dripping down my throat. *Well, that's the end of letting my feelings get in the way of being aware of my surroundings*, I told myself, standing up as soon as my nose stopped bleeding. *Did we land somewhere? A base . . . a town . . . or in the middle of the wilderness for no reason?* I hurried to grab my now scuffed helmet off the floor of the small space and tried to rub the scuff off.

Without warning, the export pad door dropped down slowly, revealing a tall tower rising kilometres into the sky, reaching the clouds effortlessly. *One tower, in the middle of a plateau with furious turbulent winds. And the ship stopped here of all places?*

What happened next almost made me think I was going crazy, because the metal cylinders simply got up and hovered down the ramp to enter a tube that followed the edge of the tower all the way up. I jogged out of the way as one of them almost pushed me over. *I've lost my mind . . . no . . . I don't know that! I couldn't have hit that hard,* I reassured myself. I reached out to touch one of the cylinders and was shocked again.

"Ow!" I exclaimed as the shock traveled all through my body sharply. *Why does everything keep shocking me?* The export pad was closing once again, and I had to quickly jump out onto the crusty, sand-like snow as the craft took off back in the direction it had come. *Did I miss something in that fort? Was there a hidden door or tube like on the side of this tower? Man, am I ever futile!* I was hard on myself, but that was how my father thought of me. Way too gullible and sensitive or . . . *defective.* I heaved a small sigh and put my fibreglass helmet back on.

"Warning! Blizzard imminent!" my small earpiece said without warning, piercing my eardrums.

"Owww! Well, isn't that obvious! We're in the blizzard region!" I yelled back. *Of course, she only wants what's best for my well being. Which does not include literally making me deaf!* I thought, frustrated with my now ringing ears. *As if I was a two-year-old and couldn't figure these things out myself. Stupid automated earpiece!*

I could see the storm, blustering in the distance.

CHAPTER 4

I crossed my arms over my chest tightly as I peered up to the top of the tower, my thoughts obnoxiously interrupted every few minutes by my automated warning system.

Cass, my automated assistant, wasn't the most helpful at times. Sure she could crunch numbers, pick the fastest route to a fueling station, and fire off texts, but really, she might be a little quieter and not such a big mouth.

Her mouth is bigger than her ears is all I'm trying to say.

She was also my birthday present from my mother two years ago.

"May I suggest a route?" she asked in her sweet, slight monotone.

"Fine, go ahead," I replied as I loaded my gun, just in case. There was no stopping Cass from voicing her opinion, plus, maybe her idea wouldn't be that bad.

"May I suggest using one of the import tubes going up the side of the storage tower?" she asked as I stiffened against the breeze, the wind howling as it got under the sealant in my airsealed suit.

"No, no, no, bad idea. Baaad, bad idea, Cass."

"If you're planning to shoot a hole in the side of the building, it will either cause a rupture in the structure's integrity," she paused, "Or it will bounce right back at you. In which case, considering the options—for comedic reasons—I'm leaning towards the latter."

"Fine, but when I shoot a hole in this thing and it stays standing I hope your circuits burn out." I flipped my gun out of the safety position and pointed it at the wall in front of me. *Let's hope plasma is strong enough . . .*

You'd think there would be no such thing as peer pressure from your personal A.I. system. But I still felt something along the lines of "if I fail the whole world will know."

I aimed, breathed out, and pulled the trigger.

The shot bounced back and hit me in the chest, making me keel over on my butt in the snow.

It bounced back at the tower, then off it, and then flew out of the atmosphere overhead in a yellow spiral. *Like a screaming firework,* I thought as I tried to re-activate my diaphram, wincing and gagging.

Cass let out an automated laugh. "Scans show the bottom half of the building is coated with an exterior layer of an unknown deflective particle barrier," she snorted as she held back another snicker. "Would you like to try again, Trigger Finger?"

"One more joke out of you and I'll drain your battery and stuff you with snow," I wheezed, rubbing my chest as I picked myself up.

One thing about Cacadin that I thought was cool was that anyone was allowed to carry around guns. And to counteract the possible outbreak of gun fights, our suits, uniform or not, could deflect Cacadin's choices in ammo, from uranium, plasma, and crystalite to electric shocks. In order for the suits to recognize the ammo, they had a membrane layer—like the connections in a brain or in our solar system—to detect the binary code embedded in the projectile.

"Jensen?"

"What, Cass?" I barked as I tried to think, pacing the length of the tower slowly. This thing was massive. By the time I walked from one end to the other I'd done six hundred and thirty meters. *What if I snuck in a vent? No, I don't think that would work, maybe for thirteen-year-old Jasper, not for me.* I sighed.

My X-ray vision turned on and Cass spoke, "I found an entrance, a large man door about fifty meters up this side of the tower. It might not be the best option when your jetpack literally hates you, but it might work," she suggested. I gazed up and spotted the door she meant.

Behind the wall there was a staircase, and the supports on both sides of the door showed up as a thick, verdigris blue. "I'm thinking anything will be better than that storm . . ."

"You're right for once, Cass. I don't want to huddle up at the base of an alien building when I can hide in the warmth," She lowered the height vision lenses. "Okay, maybe there's no warmth but at least the air is calm. Right?"

"Roger that," she replied.

For a machine she had a moderately complex grammar database.

I inhaled deeply, then pushed by breath out through my mouth. The jetpack escaped its case and lifted me off the ground quickly, ascending more steadily than I would ever have hoped.

"Cass," I initiated.

"Jetpack signatures normal," she informed me. Another slightly clear box showed up on the lens, this time showing the numbers of the jetpack's energy signatures hardly fluctuating.

I kicked the door with the heel of my boot but it didn't do anything but rattle my bones.

I kicked again.

Same reaction.

I tapped the pallet on my wrist and aimed my grappling hook upwards to a seam in the building's metal surface.

It latched on, the hooked end morphing into a stream-lined magnet.

This was one of the many things Tesla had taught me when climbing something: always have a strong wire attached above you just in case your plan fails, and always have three points of pressure on the surface. I usually ignore those types of things because, for one, I'm probably gonna die, and two, I never took the provided safety classes.

I turned off my jet, the powerful metal component fleeing back into the shell on my back.

I readied myself for impact and landed with a jolt.

I changed my stance on the side of the building, stiffening as I jumped as far out as possible.

I landed back down and dented the door.

I did it again, this time it wrinkled like tinfoil. *One more time!* My heart was racing and my legs felt like jelly as the wind blew on me, the storm growing closer with every breath.

I jumped one last time, sending every last sliver of strength I had into my long, powerful legs.

Time seemed to stop, my vision disappeared against the sudden rush and abruptness of the impact.

I blasted through the wall onto my back on the floor, my wire retracting back into the spool on my wrist as I let it go limp above my head. "It worked!" my voice cracked against the dry air.

I picked myself up and gazed down at the snowy plateau, throwing my fists up as I chanted, "Yah! That'll teach you not to mess with a *captain*, Annoterra!" A grin curled across my lips as I peered down the side of the building, wisps of wind carrying the sawdust-like snow with it.

I chuckled as I took off my helmet, my eyes escaping the clutches of the X-ray vision, which had been in front of my face for what seemed like decades.

"Congratulations, Jensen," Cass praised as I turned towards the spiraling metal plank stairs, finally able to scratch my itchy head. I brushed my long faux-hawk haircut back, then let it frill back into its casual, curly position.

I started to climb the stairs. "What is your plan now?" Cass asked.

"Hunker down till the storm is over, then see if there's a ship in the hangar," I answered quickly as I leapt up the steps.

I stopped at the top, and gazed around at the stacks of red cylinders. *Odd*, was my first thought, followed by *Why did they move them, then?* I pushed myself to touch one of the metal cylinders again and wasn't shocked this time. I was starting to get frustrated with this peculiar planet.

I dropped my glide shell to the floor and it made a hollow knocking sound. It emitted a light blue glow, making the room feel like a sky of ocean. *There's my backup plan . . . don't see why I would need it, though . . . there's nobody here.* I was starting to sweat in my thick exofiber suit, making it feel like a hot, moist desert. I unzipped my shelled overlayer, ready to spend at least an hour or two in the dark area.

I was shaken from my heavy doze by the sound of marching.

Metal feet.

Big, heavy masses ascending the stairs.

My eyes searched the walls for a door or staircase, besides the ones I'd just used. *Oh no, I've either been spotted or that's a patrol.* I quickly zipped my suit back up, with the marching noises getting closer and closer. I hoisted the heavy glide shell onto my back and it immediately reattached to the suit.

Readying my gun in the hope that shooting the wall might burn a hole in it, I put my helmet on and made sure it was sealed.

Abruptly the marching stopped, and my heart took a sickening lurch. *Stuck in a tower . . . only one way out . . . through molten metal.*

Suddenly a door slid open on one of the walls and from it came glowing blue gunfire. I shot at the other side of the room, hoping it would make a hole in the metal, but found it did not.

"Ugh! Does anything work around here?" I roared at the gun.

To make things worse, a bunch of robots came through the door, vigorously shooting crystalite bullets at me.

He's going to get himself killed!

I was alarmed to hear someone else's thought in my head, a sweet but distressed voice.

"Fantastic! Now I have a bigger problem!" I yelled at the robots, throwing my hands out then slapping them on my thighs, quickly dodging a poorly aimed bullet. The robots were made of more of the glossy metal, making it hard to locate them, since they were the same colour as the walls.

That bullet had made a gaping hole in the wall behind me. "Ha! Stupid robots! Whoever you work for is going to be super disappointed!" I scoffed, putting away my gun and focusing on getting the jump jets from my glide suit. Then the glide shell spewed out a white mass which formed into a large jump jet, just a little narrower than my shoulders.

I ran right for the glowing ring of metal and jumped through it. My heart sped triumphantly. The sun was starting to set in the distance, casting dark, eerie shadows on the ground by the tower. The blizzard had settled and left a newly windblown field, and beyond that, the most dangerous area in all the region, the mountains.

Without warning, one of the robots somehow shot my glide shell from fifty meters away, deactivating it permanently. A chill of horror ran down my spine as I began to plummet towards the ground.

"Oh, come on!" I rasped to the hole in the building overhead as I dropped rapidly. My pack blew out puffs of toxic smoke, filling the air with a gray-blue haze. *Could this day have gone any worse?* I thought, letting myself go limp. The robots came into view, looking down the side of the monstrous tower to watch me falling.

I closed my eyes, ready to accept my fate, when something large caught me by the neck of my suit, like a cat with a dead mouse. *I jinxed it! An animal has found me . . . I'm done for.*

But instead of being shaken back and forth like a chew toy, or simply ripped to pieces claws to mouth, I was carried gingerly. When I strained my neck around as far as I could, I saw a pair of large greenish-white antennae. And above that was a concerned, disturbed face clutching the neck of my suit.

You mean I travelled halfway across the region to save this little creature? PA. THE. TIC, something shouted, and I realized it must have been the large beast carrying me.

Is it going to eat me? Or maybe it will bury me in the snow and save me for later like a fox! A better question is, what is this thing? And why can I hear its thoughts? Maybe it's not an animal at all, because animals don't have thoughts, they live on instinct. I'd be the one to know, I'm a biologist. Maybe if I stay limp it'll drop me and I can escape, I rambled, staring at the ground listlessly.

Ugh, does this thing ever stop thinking? I heard it think.

I was suddenly very embarrassed.

That's better. As soon as I get this thing back to the cave I can deal with it, the large beast thought, going into a fast trot.

We can clearly hear each other . . . Hey! Could you by any chance put me down? And not eat—

"Oof!" The beast dropped me on my back into the hard snow. I sat up coughing, the wind knocked out of me, gazing up at the large creature.

It can hear me? it thought, both astonished and mortified, lowering its head down to my level. Its eyes were an onyx black, making them look empty, maybe even lifeless. I stood up, brushing myself off, still gazing into the eyes of the creature. I took my helmet off slowly, my ruffled hair blowing in the feeble wind. The creature jumped back, curling away from me, eyes wide.

Suddenly I noticed the robots taking aim at the creature and ran in front of it, aiming for the robots with the small gun.

I pulled the trigger within a split second, shooting one in the head and another square in the chest.

The other three retreated back into the walls of the building.

I was about to turn back around when all of a sudden I felt a warm breath on my neck.

I tensed. *Please don't eat me!* I prayed, putting away the gun.

CHAPTER 5

Aapi

I'm Aapi, the large, hard-shelled creature said, sitting down on the solid snow.

Jensen. Are you still going to bring me back to your cave and eat me? I asked, taking my broken pack off and chucking it in the snow.

I don't know, she mused. *I have a question for you, too. What are you?* Aapi asked, picking me up between her pincer-like arms and turning me around.

"Aaah! Put me down!" I demanded as I tried to get free of the stabby thingys. She set me back down and looked at me with a furrowed brow. I scratched my head, trying to find a way to explain. "Well, I'm from a planet called Earth, and my kind is called human. We have the most advanced technology in the entire system. Your planet just happens to be on the farthest outreaches of it."

You look like an Acolite! she exclaimed.

"A what?" I asked, perplexed.

What was that thing on your back? she asked, changing the subject. She poked the broken glide, which was still glowing with coals, with her speckled green pincers.

"Uh, that's my glide pack. It's supposed to help me jump from platform to platform. But it obviously failed to do its job," I said, breathing out an embarrassed laugh.

Well, no need for that. I can get from rock to rock better than any piece of junk, Aapi scoffed.

"Hey! It wasn't junk before those robots shot me out of the sky!" I yelled.

Aapi let out a loud snort, which made me realize she had gills. *You live in water?* I asked.

I choose not to live in the water, thank you very much. I'm a Canestalker, and let's leave it at that.

"Sorry . . . I didn't mean . . . my life has been in peril the entire day, which makes me feel like I'm going crazy. And I'm also dry on adrenalin so I feel really nauseous." I once again rambled, putting my hands over my temples, trying to stop my arteries from pulsing rapidly. I noticed she was staring at me nervously.

Can you at least hop on my back? she asked, lying down.

"Why? I can't sleep! I have way too many things to think about, like why they are transporting red orbs? That will leave me stumped for at least a week," I said, walking towards her.

Ok! Please settle down! she said sternly.

I grabbed my broken pack on the way by, making sure it had cooled off first.

One more question . . . how can you understand me when I'm talking? I asked as I struggled onto Aapi's back.

Jensen, I've been listening to your thoughts and dreams for well over a month, and I have managed to translate your language. Plus, I'm over twenty-five years old, she explained, heaving herself off the frigid ground.

"Hold on, what type of dreams?"

Well, there was this really vivid one of a river . . . but nothing really interesting, she replied, going into a fast trot.

"Wait, did you see one about a large blue creature attacking its own kind?" I asked, shoving my helmet back on as a chill went down my spine.

Yes, but I thought it was a figment of my imagination. Not— she cut herself off.

Not what, Aapi?

A vision, she finished, slowing to a walking pace.

Are you sure it wasn't just something the medical computer did to me? I asked, trying to deny it.

Yeah, phoo, what am I talking about? Of course, there hasn't been a vision since the massacre, she reasoned.

"Aapi? What massacre!? Ok, this is getting serious, you can't leave me without any context!" I yelled, shaking from the horror of the thought Aapi gave me, of this land soaked in blood and scorched with gunfire. Now I was caught on edge . . . how could I leave this planet with a vision?

I'm sorry Jensen, but I can not tell you about that. You have only been conscious for less than ten hours, and you have already been through more than anybody ever has in a week, Aapi warned, resuming her fast trot and ignoring the fact that I was straight up horrified.

But I've never been a part of anything big . . . except for winning the botany fair in grade five. And being the youngest person to go to Cacadin expeditions, I reflected, looking at the distant rocky peaks.

We were almost to the mountains when the first bright star came poking out, helping me cope with the nausea that was pounding in my head and gut. The day had drained me of energy, making it twice as hard to hold back my grumpy thoughts.

"How long is night around here, Aapi? I mean, I have a theory, but I don't have an explanation as to why, or anything," I asked, lying my head on Aapi's neck, feeling the smooth, shiny exoskeleton.

Hmm . . . last time I checked, our nights were about eight hours long, Aapi said.

"Ok, and also, do you have an endoskeleton as well, or just an exoskeleton?" I inquired, as my biologist side sunk into my thoughts. She didn't answer for at least ten minutes, only taking in the fresh air and trotting peacefully.

Aapi? Hello? I asked, concerned.

Huh? Sorry, Jensen. Actually, I do have an endoskeleton. But I'm not like the other Canestalkers, she said in a sad tone. She gazed off at the nearest mountain, seemingly trying to hold back an urge to cry.

I'm just glad you found me. Without you I would be dead, and without dignity. Now at least I'm alive, but still without dignity. I'm going to find out what happened to my crew—since

I'm alive, there must be some chance they are, too—and fix this prophecy thing.

Wow, you sure have been through a lot, lost your crew, got shot out into space, and now sharing thoughts telepathically with a strange beast!

"How do you know about me getting shot into space?"

I may have rummaged through your thoughts a little while you were unconscious. I'm sorry, but once I knew about this woman named Tesla I couldn't untangle myself from your past events, she apologized.

"That's ok, it's not like she's still alive anyway." I really missed Tesla, her smile, her amazing sense of direction, and most of all, her love of exploring new worlds.

Can I please *hear more about this wonderful woman? Maybe it will help you forget about those dreadful experiences,* she suggested as we entered the mouth of a broad valley.

I guess no harm can be done if I do tell. Well, she's my ship's Wayfinder, and also the one I love the most. She has no father and her mother died of cancer when she was only eight, so she was sent to live with some relatives. She has also been—

No . . . What are your thoughts about her? The majority of your dreams seem to be obsessed *with her. It's fine if you don't want to share, though. I mean it is very personal.* She weaved between some trees awkwardly, pushing shrubs over with her wide torso.

Nah, we basically share minds now, plus you're probably going to bug me about it and poke through my head until you find out. So sure, I will tell you. All the agonizingly painful memories are already dealt with anyway. I adjusted myself on Aapi's back so my groin wouldn't hurt any more than it already did from the suit. *Well, she's the absolute sweetest person I know, and the love of my life. Whenever I am stressed, her enthusiastic smile helps me get through it. Once she even did some of my work for me. She is the most sensible, knowledgeable, caring person I've ever met. And it's all because of Cacadin.*

So that's why you didn't like it when I said your glide was a piece of junk? I'm sorry, Jensen, that was insensitive of me, Aapi apologized, starting to turn uphill.

No, it's ok, I would have acted the same or worse if I was in your position.

We came to a small cave with odd stalactites hanging from the ceiling. I stared into the mouth of the cave, caught off guard by the glowing crystals growing on the odd rock shelf. I hopped off Aapi and admired her beautiful flat-tipped tail.

By the way, I didn't really catch your last name? she asked. I looked into her moonlit black eyes, taking my helmet off with a small click.

"Galantis. Jensen Galantis."

CHAPTER 6

My sleep was surprisingly peaceful, considering I had only gotten about seven hours in a chilly, low-lit cave. I was gently roused by Aapi's warm breath. I could hardly remember what had happened after I hopped off Aapi's back, so tired because I was pumped full of melatonin. All I remembered was lying down on a comfortable bed of furs. Aapi stared at me expectantly, her face lit by a large red mass in the wall by my feet.

Good morning! How was your sleep? What do humans eat nowadays? Avigulls? she asked excitedly. She acted as if she'd seen a human before. She was definitely proving she was gentle, considering she was almost sitting right on top of me and hadn't crushed me yet. I sat up and looked at her nervously, and she backed off to sit on her hindquarters.

"Umm, what's an Avigull?" I asked, stretching my sore neck by clutching it in my hands and pulling it into an arch towards my crossed legs.

Here, I'll show you. I just have to catch one first, she explained as her tail trailed out of the cave behind her. *Are you coming?*

Yeah, sure. I stood up awkwardly, spreading my arms apart as far as I could to stretch. I followed her stiffly,

43

noticing Aapi's tail was strangely similar to a creature from Earth, but I couldn't put my finger on which one.

Once outside the dark cave, we approached a steep, snowy rockface. I found it quite hard to climb with an empty stomach, but where else would we find food in this balmy, snowy terrain? *Blizzardia kind of reminds me of British Columbia*, I reflected.

Listen to Aapi, I told myself. *She was born and raised here. Besides, how bad could Avigulls taste?*

A large, bloody bird dropped right at my feet from the shelf above me and I let out a startled chuckle. I touched the headless body with one of my boots.

"Uhh, is that an Avigull, Aapi?"

Yup. I've tried to reach the nest but the shelf is too narrow. Maybe you can get to it, with your wide feet and slender torso?

"Oh, those are just my boots. But sure, I guess I can give it a shot. Don't get mad at me, though, if they start attacking me and my eyes get poked out by their beaks," I said, starting to climb to the next shelf.

Oh! Hehe, don't worry, they don't have sharp beaks, they have venomous talons that give you paralysis and make you drool. She sat underneath the shelf serenely, apparently oblivious to the fact I could die just trying to fetch breakfast. I stared across to the other side of the shelf at nests carved into the sandstone sediment.

Should I be worried about them scratching at my throat? I asked as I inched across the thin shelf towards the nests.

Nah! That's just how they protect their eggs. Also, the eggs are self-heated, so don't touch them with your bare— She was cut off by my howl as I reached out and grabbed one of the glowing red shells.

. . .*hands.* Aapi cringed.

I'm really starting to judge your teaching methods! You couldn't have told me this before I burned myself? I clutched my hand tightly as I felt the pain go all the way up my arm.

Sometimes you just have to learn the hard *way,* she thought.

I tucked my un-burnt hand in my exofiber suit, and making sure I didn't burn myself this time I plucked an egg out of the nest swiftly, hoping none of the juveniles saw. I seized a few more of the large, speckled eggs before scrambling down the shelf at the sound of a loud screech, which sent an eerie chill down my spine. A smile of delight was written across Aapi's face. The lush undergrowth brushed up against my waist lightly as we walked slowly back to the cave with tight, hungry stomachs.

"Hmm . . . Now, how are we going to cook this? I don't suppose you can breathe fire like a medieval dragon?" I inquired, scratching my head impatiently.

What? No! That isn't even genetically possible, she thought loudly, piercing my head with almost a holler.

Ugh! Ok, it was just a question! I didn't really expect you to be able to. I just thought since we speak to each other telepathically, it might somehow be possible.

Aapi scrunched up her snout, showing she did not like the idea.

"What is that glowing mass in the wall?" I asked, walking over to the radiant vermilion lump. It bulged out of the wall like a piece of molten lava, making the rock walls look more like a volcano.

It's skyrite. It holds heat extremely well, and like the Avigull eggs, it will give a second-degree burn if you touch it with your bare hands, she said.

I learned my lesson last time. Getting burned from a bird egg was probably one of the most shocking, bizarre things that had happened yet. I set the eggs down gently on a rock shelf beside me, standing them up on a few sharp crystal protrusions.

"Do you have something sharp? Like a knife or something?" I asked, inspecting the cave.

Well, some of the crystals are sharp and pointy, although I doubt you will be able to break— she began, but I suddenly materialized my blaster from the mineral casing and shot at the indigo crystals. Aapi's jaw dropped with astonishment as one of the acute crystals went tumbling to the floor, sparkling like a fire opal and sending a cascade of colours onto my black suit. I picked it up with a toothy smile.

Hey! Those Zularon crystals are not easy to find! she shouted, growling at me with a scrunched up snout.

"Do you want breakfast or not?" I glared at her, frustrated. She turned her gaze to the floor, suddenly realizing how hungry we both were, and how she could sacrifice one of her marvellous crystals for a knife.

Just don't turn my cave into a battle zone, ok? she wailed.

I won't. Didn't do it to my ship, won't do it to your cave, I promised, gesturing to the scorch mark on the wall with my gun. Aapi settled her snout back into a relaxed state and stared longingly at the eggs.

What are you going to do with the piece of skyrite? she asked, inching closer to me as I cut carefully into the bulging mass, making sure not to take off too much.

"I'm going to cook breakfast on it, obviously," I replied. "But it depends if you want me to cook yours," I said as the large piece tumbled to the ground, sizzling. Aapi gave me a disgusted look before loosening her expression to accept the offer.

Well, it's not like you're going to be with me in my cave for much longer, she said. I snapped my head to look at her quickly, absolutely shocked.

CHAPTER 7

I was about to protest when I was abruptly pinned down on the hard floor, the gun knocked out of my hand. My arm was immobilized by someone's foot, which from my angle I could not see clearly. I reached my free hand up to a black boot with a wide-rimmed bottom and realized what it was.

A Cacadin boot? I stared up in disbelief to find a tall figure glaring at me. My eyes were blurry from the loss of moisture in the deep cave air, my throat itching painfully as my breathing heaved and sped.

I was relieved to hear Aapi's deep-throated roar, which forced the figure to look up from its victim . . . in this case, me. Its skin was unearthly pale, with a slight icy tinge and a glossy coat. A few splotches glowed on its cheekbones. Aapi jumped at the mysterious character, pinning it against the far cave wall, then let out a large hiss to let the intruder know she could strike at any moment. I leapt up and grabbed my burnished black pistol off the floor, clutching it in both my hands and pointing it at the individual pinned to the wall. My careening gaze caught its sleeveless arm. Unlike the other arm, it had a cut parallel to the shoulder and a white line following that along its hidden seams. I blinked a few times to clear my blurry eyes as I suddenly realized this was someone I thought I would never see again.

Tesla. My pulse skipped.

Aapi! Stop! No, don't kill her! I thought in panic, as my hard-shelled companion was about to rip out Tesla's throat with her large white teeth. Aapi dropped her on the floor and Tesla, shaking, inched slowly away from Aapi's snarling head towards a pile of red crystals.

"Jensen, what are you doing here? You should be dead!" she shuddered.

I stood, still paralyzed from seeing my Wayfinder. *How is she still alive? Why is she here? What happened to her? Why is she so white?*

"I . . . don't know." I hadn't really thought about how I had survived. I kept staring at her.

Tell her you're the Pre-Sighter, Aapi told me, staring at Tesla.

Pre-Sighter? What's that, exactly? I asked, my interest growing.

She snorted internally. *It means you can see multiple possibilities for the close future. You* can *do that, right?* She swivelled her head to peer at me expectantly.

Pfft! How am I supposed to know what I can do, Aapi? My favorite person in literally the entire universe is right here in front of me, and almost bleached white of all things! You found me, so that means there's a reason for us being tethered and for you to think I'm some Pre-Sighter, too. The fingers on my left hand curled into a fist, knuckles flushing at my side. I swallowed my feelings, pushing down my internal struggles.

I turned my gaze back to Tesla. "How are *you* still alive?" I asked as my eyes filled with tears. "Where are the others?"

I took a few anxious steps towards her as she gazed back at me.

"The Rebels found me floating in the atmosphere," she answered, her breathing settling. "If you want to hear it all, I was kept in a cell, observed and tested. But luckily they were able to return me to my normal self. They still don't trust a hybrid." She paused, choking on her next words. "But a few weeks later, one of Nixon's armies attacked our base. If it weren't for me they wouldn't be dead under a mountain. So, my only way to show the Rebels I was worthy enough to be trusted as a Lieutenant was to find the Pre-Sighter. I've been tracking the energy signature with my beacon . . . for days." The odd glowing patches on her cheeks and neck pulsed rapidly.

An Acolite? How is she a hybrid? She's been through more than I have!

"Whoa, whoa, whoa. Okay, slow down. How powerful is this Nixon guy?" I asked, kneeling beside her and taking her bare arm gently, spooked by the immense amount of heat her body gave off.

"He's an Acolite who enslaves the minds of his own people, putting them into computers to use them over and over again, like the system that our grandparents used when they were kids. What was it, Google? The computer is linked to a big hard drive somewhere and loops the Acolites around when their server on the other end gets destroyed."

I was filled with horror at the idea that, somehow, knowledge like that made it all the way across the system. *This is bigger than I thought,* I mused while staring down at the gray floor, trying to process all the information Tesla was briskly spewing out.

She stood up quickly and I let go of her arm.

"But . . . Dax, Arron, Jasper and the cadets are nowhere to be found, either frozen in space or caught by Nixon," she finished.

That wasn't surprising. It was already a miracle that Tesla and I had survived. I still felt the vast pain of being responsible for those lives. I had trained them to be some of the best cadets in the galaxy.

I ran my fingers through my hair gently, realizing how knotty it was.

"I might have been unconscious this entire time, memories put into a medical machine, escaped to a tower, attacked by a bunch of robot crystalite bullet snipers, and found by Aapi, thanks for asking." My throat seized up, hearing that my memories were now in the hands of a bloodthirsty monster.

What are you going to tell her about the vision? Aapi interjected, nudging me with her snout.

"Aapi, I have literally no idea!"

"You can hear that thing? Jensen, you're friends with the apex predator?" she asked nervously. I clutched her hand in mine, not even caring how badly burned I was.

You're an apex predator? You never cease to amaze me! I thought, impressed with Aapi's surprising impact on Blizzardia's food chain.

Well, yes. I've never eaten an Acolite before, though, she mused.

I thought maybe she still hated Tesla for some odd reason. But, did it really matter at the moment? No.

"Technically she's friends with me, she found me, she saved me. Aapi's been surfing through my dreams and memories ever since I was captured," I said, rubbing Aapi's head. Tesla suddenly tried to let go of my hand.

"Are you crazy? You share thoughts with this beast?" She used her other hand to try to pry mine off.

"Tesla, trust me, you're fine, this is the safest place to be." I kept my grip on her. She stopped her squirming when I said, "I'm the Pre-Sighter."

CHAPTER 8

Nordic T

Tesla's eyes turned entirely black as she pulled a large gun out of her Cacadin holster. I rolled out of the way as she attempted to shoot me and ended up turning the Avigull eggs into scorched flakes..

What happened to her? I glared at her frightening appearance, repelled.

I ran towards Tesla and tackled her, knocking the breath out of her lungs as we slammed onto the floor.

"*Aapi, run!*" I rasped as Tesla attempted to kick me in the stomach with one of her heavy boots and barely missed. Aapi raced out of the cave as fast as she could, not looking back.

Suddenly, a large flaming, serrated knife extended from Tesla's sleeved arm. I avoided the first swing, but the red hot blade lashed back for another attack and made a deep gash from the top of my nose to the bottom of my right jawbone, sending a gush of blood onto the floor. I released my grip from her shoulders as I stumbled backward, reaching one of my shaky hands up to feel my burnt and bloody face.

The delayed pain suddenly shot through my skull. Tesla hopped back onto her feet, now pointing her oversized gun at me.

My vision blurred with anger and revulsion, I pulled my gun out of my holster. Without even thinking about what I was doing, I let the rage take over and pointed the gun at Tesla.

"You can't kill me! If you try, your friend here dies instead!" Tesla sneered, firing her gun at the ceiling above me. I jumped out of the way as razor-sharp stalactites came tumbling to the floor with a loud crash.

As I lay there, my rage receded as I suddenly realized it wasn't Tesla attempting the assault, she was in fact possessed by someone. My eyes opened wide with horror and I clenched my fists from the pain and disorientation that flooded over me. My sore face pulsated relentlessly, trying to clot the deep wound. My lower half felt like jelly. The blood slowly dripped from my face, giving the impression of tears as it slid past my eyes.

"I would never hurt you, I'm only trying to help you," I winced as I picked myself up off the hard ground, my breathing shallow. "Whatever this person is doing to you, fight it as long as you can. Don't give up. Don't do what I did so many times over." My vision became more obscured and clouded.

"Hahaha! You can't get her back! I have been planning to kill you for years. There is no escaping your blood-soaked fate!" the mysterious voice said.

"And the best part of it all, I don't need an army to do it." Tesla, still possessed, chucked her gun on the ground and strode over to me to finish the job.

No, I won't let you kill me! I thought, sweeping her off of her feet and tying her up with my wire.

"You're stronger than I expected!" the strange voice hissed in anger. The blood continued to drip onto my suit as I tried to tie the knot securely. Her eyes suddenly shifted to their normal, violent purple colour, then pulsed black once more, returning with the attacker's cold voice.

"You've won this time, Galantis! But you can't protect the ones you love forever."

I shuddered as the mysterious presence disappeared from her consciousness. Tesla let out a cough and gasped as if she had been drowning in water this entire time.

"Ugh, my head hurts! What happened? Jensen, why am I tied up?" I crouched beside her, brushing a piece of blond hair out of her face.

She lifted her head to meet my eyes, and I looked away quickly so I could spare myself the pain of watching her look at my face. "Jensen . . . your face. Did I do that?" I nodded slowly, letting the blood trickle onto the floor as I untied the hiking knot and grabbed back the wire.

"It doesn't matter. We need to find Aapi," I said, helping her up off the ground. I grabbed my helmet and put my gun back into the canister as I headed towards the mouth of the cave.

"Do you think she went to the Rebels?" Tesla asked, grasping my hand.

"Depends. If she knows what's best for her, then yes. If she's being the jumpy, disorientated maniac who woke me up this morning, then she probably found a tree to hide under." I touched my tingling face and winced. Tesla wiped off an oozing line of blood as it tried to dribble into my mouth.

"So, what was with the ominous person in your head?" I asked.

"Long story short, that's Nixon, and he wants to kill you," she replied.

CHAPTER 9

"Huh … well, it isn't the worst quality in the world," I admitted, pulling her closer to me.

"I'm not joking, this is going to get you killed one day!" she warned.

I had seen the proof first hand.

"I have to admit, though, you're better at fighting than I thought!" I cackled. My cut was clotted now and I could finally move my face a little more freely. It still felt like a bunch of tiny needles piercing my face, but it was better than being dead on the floor.

"Hey, can't you just talk to her telepathically?" she asked, gesturing to my head.

Why didn't I think of that?

"Umm, yes, I can try," I answered, pushing everything else out of my head.

Aapi, please answer if you can hear me. After a few moments, I sighed and scratched my head, trying to think of another way to find her.

"You said that your beacon tracks the energy signature of the Pre-Sighter, right?" I asked, looking out at the towering trees.

"Yes, but I'm not sure if it will track—"

"We need to try," I cut her off. She pulled out a large opal-like cube and held it out in her hand. It looked as if it had been scratched, then another coat of stone put on top of it, then scratched again, with that process repeated over and over again until it was a cube. "What is that?" I asked, reaching out to touch it when she slapped my hand.

"It's an Undorian crystal, it vibrates with different energy concentrations." She twirled the small cube in her palm. "Anything that is Acolite can explode from your energy signature. The Pre-Sighter, being the strongest, might be used as an explosive if you touch it. So whatever you do, do not touch it," she said sternly. "We can see if it will work for Aapi, but you will have to concentrate all your energy towards her," she explained, walking closer to the cave entrance, while still far enough away to avoid the fluffy snowflakes that were falling outside.

Venomous clawed birds, burning hot eggs, glowing swelter-ing masses, and now stuff can explode at will? I'm starting to doubt Cacadin knows how safe this planet really is, I thought.

"Hello? Jensen, I need you to concentrate," Tesla said, waving her hand in front of my face.

"Sorry," I apologized. I focused my thoughts relentlessly on Aapi and the things she had done for me.

The cube vibrated slightly, in a low, almost impercep-tible frequency.

"It's faint, but I think it worked," she said, scratching the back of her head and making her long blond braid swish back and forth.

"Jensen, can you grab my gun?" she asked as the cube started to pull against her grip. I reached over to pick up the glowing purple gun and a small string of electricity jumped onto my hand and up my arm. I let out a growl as I grasped it forcefully.

"Why does your Acolite tech keep shocking me all the time?" I blurted as I put the gun back in her holster.

"It's because you're the Pre-Sighter, genius! Like I said, weird energy signature, extremely conductive!" she explained as the cube almost knocked her off her feet.

"As soon as I let this cube go, it's going to shoot out of the cave." She adjusted her grip. "Does your glide still work? Actually, I see it over there, definitely doesn't work. You know what, use mine."

"But how are you going to get there?" I asked, detaching the glowing purple shell from her back.

"Jensen, just do it!" she replied. I attached the large pack to the slots on the heated spine of my suit, and the pack's glowing spots turned a stunning cyan blue.

"Huh, didn't expect that would work," I said, trying to see the pack a little closer. Tesla looked at me with a how-dare-you-doubt-me look and I unfolded the jet to avoid further negative expressions.

"Ready?" Tesla asked, putting all her weight onto the cube as it dragged her a little further. I threw my helmet on and got into position.

"Yeah." She let go of the cube and I shot out of the cave behind it, snowflakes banging on the glass. I quickly avoided a towering tree as the cube banged into it, sending a mixture of snow and needles into the air.

I came to a sudden stop as I realized where the cube was going, what I may have done to Aapi.

A shadow I assumed was just the sun getting blocked by dense clouds came over me. But I was startled to learn the shadow wasn't a cloud when a figure abruptly landed on me from above, and we started to fall towards the ground.

At first I assumed it was a griffin or small dragon, but was astonished to find it was actually Tesla. She waved as I looked at her angrily, trying to maneuver myself vertically to stop us from plummeting.

Ok, *where the heck did she come from?* I thought, centering myself just in time to prevent us smashing into the ground. I landed slowly, letting Tesla hop off my back shakily.

I unclipped my helmet from my bloody collar, set it into the helmet slot of my suit, and stared at Tesla expectantly. She inched a foot or two away from me, realizing she could have gotten us both killed.

"Umm, sorry, Jensen." She lowered her head slightly.

"It's ok. Did you just fall from the sky?" I asked, looking to the heavens, imagining I would find a platform or a hovering object. She avoided my eyes as if she didn't want to answer. The lanky trees waved in the strong winds that whistled through the narrow valley, sending icy snow into our hair and faces.

"Did you find her?" I gazed off at a massive cave in the large rock face, hoping the beacon had accidentally miscalculated.

"Yes," her gaze shifted towards me. "But I'm not sure how easy it will be to get her back."

CHAPTER 10

I jumped from rock to rock as I tried to climb the treacherous slab shelf to the cave, praying I wouldn't die trying to save my telepathic "pet" from the clutches of a mysterious monster.

By the time I heaved myself onto the level ground, Tesla was waiting there, trying to stay as quiet and low-lit as possible.

"How do we even know there is a large perilous beast in there, waiting to eat us?" she asked quietly. As an answer, I pointed to a pile of pearly white rib bones by the cave entrance.

"How did you get up here so quickly?" I asked, trying to catch my breath. Again she didn't answer.

"Tesla? If you don't want to share, that's fine. I'm just curious."

She will probably share at the appropriate time . . . just wait patiently, I told myself, inching closer to the cave entrance.

"Tesla, if I die, you can be captain." Tesla looked at me anxiously, waiting to see if I was joking or not. I let out a low chuckle as I peeked my head in the cave. I waved my hand at Tesla to beckon her into the cave.

"I found the beacon . . . sort of." I peered over to see a heaving mass in the corner, with the glass-like beacon in between its powerful jaws. I wrinkled my bumpy nose as I took in a whiff of the horrible, rotting stench.

"Jensen, are you serious? You're sure you want to follow through with this?" she whispered, backing hastily towards the entrance.

"Oh, grow up! It's not going to wake up if we're quiet," I assured her. "Let's just find Aapi and get out of here."

"Unstable cave system ahead," my earbuds blurted, once again piercing my eardrums. I pried them from my swollen ears, tearing the magnet from the cartilage of my ear. The magnets in the earbuds were attracted to another small magnet in the top half of my ears under the skin, implanted the day after I got them.

"Why can't you just stay a consistent volume already?" I complained as quietly as possible.

And now I'm talking to an inanimate object, perfect. I muted the earbuds and put them back in. Then, with my helmet back on, I peeked my head around a corner to find Aapi cocooned in glowing green silk. I stared at her for a few moments, then realized what she reminded me of.

"Psst! Hey, crayfish!" I whispered. Aapi opened her eyes slowly.

What are you doing here? That Kerosene Lion is going to slaughter you! she warned, nudging me with her snout, almost pushing me over.

What in Gagarin's name is a Kerosene Lion? That's a common Terran fuel from Earth!

The common theme is hot, glowing, and poison. Why do you think it's called that? she snapped.

I tugged on the thick silk, trying to break it with my bare hands.

"Tesla, I found her." Abruptly she appeared behind me, staring at Aapi narrowly. "Ok then, Tesla can I have your knife, please?" I held out my hand as I looked closer at the incredibly strong silk.

Tesla unlocked the serrated, vermilion hot blade from her sleeve and handed it to me carefully. The knife cut through the silk effortlessly, giving off small sizzling noises.

"Umm, Jensen . . . you might want to turn around." She shook my shoulder, making me miss the thick strands.

"Tesla, I'm almost done! Just—" I turned to find myself face to face with the most dangerous thing in the region. It breathed a hot, moist breath on my face, blowing my hair into my eyes.

"Jensen, what now?" Tesla whispered frantically, grasping my hand.

"You run . . . Aapi and I will distract it," I whispered into her ear. "Hand me your gun and I'll try to shoot it. That shouldn't be too hard, right?" I scrutinized her. "Right?" The beast let out a snort and Tesla jerked back.

"I think we should just run," she replied as the lion turned its gaze back towards me.

"And let it tie us up too? No way, Tesla, we have to find some way that this thing won't chase after us!"

"You're not going to be able to shoot that thing," she replied, putting her hand over the canister as I was about to grab it.

"Ugh! Why not?" I debated with her, staring at the glowing red creature.

"It has armour, much like Aapi, that is impenetrable to these small blasters."

Small? I stopped that thought as I had a great idea.

"Hey Tesla, what if we shot the rock shelf above the cave entrance? Would that cause the arch to collapse on itself?" I asked, shifting to huddle closer beside Tesla. "Would it lock the lion inside?"

I'm just glad this thing has a blind spot!

"You sane captain!" she exclaimed proudly, "But how are we going to get past it without getting caught in the paralyzing silk?"

"Paralyzing? Does that mean Aapi can't move?" I asked impatiently, taking a worried glance at Aapi.

"No, it only lasts for a few minutes, long enough for the lion to either eat its prey . . . or save it for later," she answered.

I shuddered.

"I think we better move if we want to get out alive." I pointed to the entrance. Tesla nodded, then threw a small pebble at the other cave wall. The lion shot around and we ran as fast as we could. I was relieved to see Aapi following behind, wagging her head to get the strings off her ears.

"Tesla, hand me your gun!" I shouted as the beast came right for us. I almost dropped the weapon and Tesla snickered. I blasted, and without warning the rock shelf above the entrance came crashing down on the beast as it let out a loud, agonized shriek.

"Space has made you a little weak, eh? Should have gotten out of the office more," she giggled as we all sat down. I chuckled, throwing my helmet onto a bank of snow.

"Holy! That thing is heavy!" I exclaimed, examining the gun.

It's weird . . . I don't have any recollection of the events that just happened. Aapi plopped down in the snow beside us. *Jen, could you tell me?*

Sure.

CHAPTER 11

Tesla stared at me horror-struck.

I put my hand on her shoulder, trying to comfort her.

"I didn't mean to, Jensen. I would never . . ." she trailed off, setting her forehead on her arms to look down at the snow between her legs.

"Tesla, it's fine, it wasn't you," I said, once again touching my clotted face.

So what are you guys? Friends? Husband and wife? Captain and Wayfinder? Co-workers? Aapi asked.

"What? Umm, I don't know. Definitely not married, though," I answered, causing Tesla to look up from her sob for a few seconds. I stared off at the sun, which was high in the sky, wondering if Tesla and I would ever get married. *Our lives have just started, give it time.* "I guess we're just friends?" I gazed at Tesla, waiting for her to answer, but she didn't reply.

"Tesla, there isn't anything to worry about. This will heal," I pointed to my face. "And Nixon won't be able to hurt anyone else but me." She lifted her gaze to meet mine as she dried her tears.

I don't care if I have this scar for the rest of my short, meaningless life. I'm going to protect Tesla, I thought determinedly. I scratched a sudden itch, and was shocked to feel the wound go down my neck too. I let out a frustrated sigh, but left it at that, so I wouldn't damage Tesla's feelings even more. *That could have ended even worse if she hadn't had a flaming blade!* I thought, for once thankful for something that hurt me.

"I don't think we should go find the Rebels," Tesla mumbled quietly, looking up at me.

"Why? Because of Nixon?"

"No, because I'm not sure how the council will react when I bring the core the problem to them." She gave me an I-don't-want-you-to-die look, and I blushed. "They would probably try to kill you and me. All I'm saying is, we could camp for a few nights somewhere, then go to the new base," she said as she drew an avalanche sign in the fluffy snow with her pointer finger.

"How do you know where the base is?" I asked.

"Anyone who leaves the base has a tracker in either their clothes or skin. And whenever they need to get back, they just tap the small computer chip and it will show a map," she explained, rubbing away the last of her tears and tapping her uncovered wrist. I gazed up at something that looked more like wires strung along nails than a map, but it made a lot of sense. Green for the most recent track and purple for the least recent.

"So, you're an Acolite. What do red, blue and yellow wires mean?" I asked, shifting my position from clutching-my-legs-in-my-arms-ouch-tailbone to cross-legged. Tesla tapped the chip embedded in her wrist again and gazed at me with clouded eyes.

"They store the Acolites, the lost Rebels, and innocent children. We've been working on a virus to override the system for months, but every one of them has failed," she said forlornly.

I stood up and walked over to her, then knelt down to look her in the eyes. "They won't suffer while I'm still here. If this is what I was meant to do, I can save them." She peered at me for a moment before hugging me.

"The universe was right about you. I will be by your side the entire time, no matter how hard things get!" she reassured me. I hugged her back and my heart skipped.

I suddenly felt Aapi's warm saliva slide up the side of my face.

"Aww! Aapi!" She gave a deep-throated cackle as I wiped the carcass-smelling drool off my cheek. Tesla let go of me and giggled, looking at Aapi's green snout. I stood up, trying to get the drool off as it stuck to my hand now. Back and forth and back and aw yuck! *You've won this time, saliva! Now I have to wash my suit!*

"So, where now?" I asked, splattering the remaining saliva on Aapi then walking closer to the rocky cliff.

"Camp out, travel, go find the base." Tesla picked a piece of dirt off my blue highlighted suit. "Go to the core of Hebion territory and free the Acolites. Your choice, Pre-Sighter. I would suggest the former though," she said.

"Hard decision. I don't know, what do you think, Aapi?" I asked looking over at Aapi's splattered body.

I suggest we travel till sundown. Where? I don't know, Aapi offered.

"North then? Deeper into the mountains, where it's balmy. Then we can find the base." I pointed towards a mountain range that looked like it just had a temper tantrum, much like me.

"Hehe! North is over there!" Tesla pushed my arm to the right with her pointer finger. "I really think you should have gotten out of the office!" she said, messing up my knotty hair more than it already was.

"Aaa! Tesla, I told you to stop doing that!" I quickly patted my hair back down, then teased her back by flipping her heavy braid over her face. She swung it back to hang over her shoulder, sending a few short hairs into her face.

"Lead on, Captain Jensen Galantis," she beamed, hopping on to Aapi's back. "Noble steed! We must trot as fast as we can!" she exclaimed. I put the oversized gun in my holster and grabbed my helmet. Then I hopped onto Aapi's back in front of Tesla, trying to find a way to grip the smooth shell.

CHAPTER 12

Was that Aapi or Tesla talking? I couldn't tell anymore. The thousand questions that now clouded my mind and ears were excruciating.

How did the tarragon plant escape?

"Why did you hide in the tower?"

How did you fall off the tower?

"Why didn't you fight back against me?"

"Guys! Can you please settle down?" I asked in a hoarse voice, glaring back and forth between them.

"I mean, could we do one question at a time?"

"Sure? Sorry, were we both talking again?" Tesla asked.

When was the last time I had a shower? It was a week before we got attacked and then a month after we crashed . Wow. I resisted smelling my armpit. *I'm glad this suit is air sealed.*

"So, why did you hide in the tower?" Tesla asked, adjusting herself.

I remembered the raging stormfront. There had been no other choice, no bike, no other form of shelter.

"There was a blizzard about to hit the area, no other deciding factor." I pushed a small branch out of the way before it hit my face.

"When I heard the soldiers approaching, I froze. I relied too much on my gun, instead of finding a way to escape without being seen." I once again looked up at the sun, which was glowing a deep orange-gold on the horizon.

I told you, you were going to get yourself killed! Aapi shouted.

"Yes, but most people don't have a telepathic connection to a crayfish. I found it quite disturbing." Aapi craned her neck to grab me off her back and dropped me, once again, on my back in the snow. I let out a small cough as I got up and brushed myself off.

You listen up, Jensen. I was created by Nixon to have telepathic abilities. This is his war, that's his puppet. She flicked one of her antennae at Tesla. *You're his pawn. I'm the one resisting him. Without me, you're doomed to a fate of destroying our galaxy.* She poked me with one of her pincers, knocking me backwards.

"Wait, back up, I'm his pawn?" I asked, shocked. She ignored my question.

Another secret! And if you have a problem with all of that, then go find a spaceship and go back to your polluted planet of misery, she said resentfully. She flicked her tail back and forth, showing how irritated she really was.

"Don't take this the wrong way, Aapi. I know this isn't my war. But I'm staying here, to defend this planet. I have nothing to go back to, I'll be the worst pilot in the entire system." I looked into her eyes. "I would be all over the news: Captain Jensen Keaton Galantis, cadets, mechanics, Wayfinder, weapons specialist, frozen to a crisp in outer space. Accusation: ejecting his crew into a war zone." My eyes clouded with pain.

Good point, she said, calming down.

"I think we should camp here for the night." I peered around at our surroundings: the long shadows under the Jack Pine-like trees, the icy melted snow plastered to them, and the multi-coloured needles that lay on the ground. "We're obviously all tired and sore. I know I'm hungry. Not sure about you guys, but I might go find an Avigull nest."

I was too emotional to be around anyone right now, which was mostly an excuse. I dropped my helmet in the snow by a large stump and turned towards the bushes. This time I didn't care if my music fried my eardrums. I started to climb a vertical rock face when I abruptly felt something grasp my arm. I spun around to find Tesla's kind eyes looking into mine. I softened my harsh expression, realizing how upset I was, turned down my music, and hopped down from the sandstone outcrop.

"Jensen . . ." She read the emotions on my face. "I know how much you're hurting, but if you keep dwelling on the past, the future won't be any better." She continued to stare into my eyes, making it twice as hard to keep all my mixed emotions from spewing out. "It's ok to grieve, but don't let them change the way you think, the way you talk, the way you act."

I didn't know how to react. I'd never had someone use such a hushed, calm, convincing voice. She started to walk away, but I knew instinctively what to do.

"Tesla." She stopped and turned back to look at me. "I'm sorry about the past few years. I haven't been there for you like you have been for me," I croaked as my throat swelled. I picked at one of my fingernails, trying my hardest to keep my emotions in check. "But if I could fix it, like you said,

I would have to do it in the present." I walked closer to her and reached for her hand, grasping it lightly. "Please stay with me. I love you like the stars in the sky." I pulled her closer to me, feeling her smooth face. "I don't care if I'm surrounded by aliens, or if I take a bullet to the chest." I gave her a small, elegant kiss. "I'm going to protect you."

"It's not 'like the stars in the sky,' it's 'as much as the number of stars in the sky,'" she giggled with tears in her eyes.

"Yeah, I suck at poetry," I joked, shrugging.

We were interrupted by a loud crash, followed by Aapi's raging battle roar and a resounding thud.

Oh, what now? Can't we have one *day where there isn't something horrible going on?* But what I saw was heart-stopping, straight up horrifying. Lying limp on the ground was Aapi, the one thing that I thought was indestructible.

CHAPTER 13

I gazed down at Aapi's limp body, blood seeping out of her neck. My eyes filled with tears as my head snapped up to meet the eyes of a teal-skinned Acolite, and I realized who it was. The square markings on his face were unmistakable.

"What is wrong with you, Nixon? Killing my team in space, locking me in a room attached to a table, destroying the Rebel base?" I yelled at him.

His pompous look was tormenting. How could someone be so self-centered?

I noticed his bloody sword. So many things didn't make sense: trying to kill Aapi, enslaving his own kind . . . What was I missing? He let out a small chuckle and I felt a heart-stopping prickle on my back.

"You're so fun to play with!" he said through Tesla's possessed body, trying to get a rise out of me. "I could just kill you, Jensen. But what would be the fun in that? So tell me," he paused as he forced Tesla to twirl the knife painfully on my backbone. I felt the threads of my suit tear under the sharp pressure of the blazing knife Tesla held in her possessed hand.

Make your move and I'll make mine . . .

"What is your plan for reversing your father's mess, hmm? To create a world so much like your filthy, cursed planet?" he continued.

I winced. I had always assumed my father used his advanced knowledge to create a planet free of poison and corruption. The accusation that this was not true felt like a dagger through the heart. I tried to keep my voice from cracking as I pushed bravery from my lungs, "I'm not telling you anything. Just kill me and leave Tesla alone."

"Tesla is nothing but my outwitted puppet, my sub-weapon of a daughter."

My stomach took a horrible lurch. Since when was Tesla's father the mastermind of war? Tesla had said her father had been a Ukrainian who worked for the Canadian Marine Corp, not an Acolite with a monstrous lust for blood. He could clearly see the shock written on my face, which apparently was what he wanted. A toothy smile spewed across his face. "If you want your precious crab to live, then you better start talking." Nixon pointed the wide sword at Aapi's seized-up body, then stabbed the blade into the ground beside her snout.

Let Aapi suffer, or tell him everything so I can save my friends . . . how helpful, I thought resentfully.

Jensen, don't do this! Aapi pleaded, opening her eyes slightly.

I have to. You and Tes mean too much to me. Tesla lowered the knife as I knelt by Aapi's head, trying to calm her racing, shallow breath.

"I'll do whatever you want, just let me help her. I'm nothing without Aapi."

Nixon snorted loudly before releasing Tesla from his trance. I caught her, watching her eyes flicker as if they were holograms that had lost their source.

We need to stop Aapi from bleeding . . . What can I use that holds moisture but acts like fibers? I set Tesla beside Aapi and looked around frantically. There was a growth on the trees that looked like the lichen I knew as old man's beard. I raced over to a large cedar-like tree and picked off a generous amount, then pelted back past the pool of cyan blood that dripped from Aapi's thick neck.

I dabbed off-black, moss-like substance on the shallow cut that ran down her neck and across her underbelly. If she was lucky, the gash would heal without any major damage, leaving only a surface scar. She flinched as I pulled a large needle out of a case hidden on my calf.

"Hey, no, it's ok, just hold on," I soothed as I pushed the syringe of anesthesia into her, hoping it would work. It's not like anyone has ever tried to sedate a crayfish, right?

"I've got one more question for you, Nixon. Why did you try to kill Aapi?"

"She betrayed me, eleven years ago during the massacre." He crossed his arms, staring at a pair of birds that hopped happily from branch to branch.

"And that would make you—"

"But unless you want to die, you better keep to your own problems," he threatened.

"I would never have expected you of all people to be Tesla's father," I said under my breath, tying the moss to Aapi's neck with a piece of wire from my grappling hook. I stood up and moved over to him slowly, then realized how much taller he was than me. I was six foot seven, and he had to be seven feet.

I noticed his gray vest, fitted with pockets and zippers, and his rich black elbow-length shirt with sharp grey icicle-like decal designs. Square markings ran all the way down his arms to his wrists, giving a slightly tiger-like effect. His pants were somewhat baggy, made of a sturdy cloth, and fitted with more pockets and a grey holster which held an odd, almost rifle-like pistol. It looked as if it could be unfolded to create a much bigger, bulkier ACR. The small case on his thigh was also unmistakeable, it held some form of daggers. He definitely looked prepared to face an army of Rebels.

By the time I finished explaining to Nixon everything I knew about Earth, Cacadin, and what I was going to do about the war, Tesla was sitting close to the small fire with a flushed, disturbed face. I glanced over at Aapi to see her still asleep, but her breathing had slowed and was deep.

"And I suppose you still want to kill me? For what, though?" I asked, lowering my gaze to the fire and scratching my head.

"Just look at your wrist," he gestured to my left arm with one of his freckled hands. I rolled up the thick fabric to reveal blue triangles in a ring all the way around.

"Like Aapi said, you're my pawn, the most powerful weapon in the entire universe. But you still have a mind of your own and could kill me at any second," he replied. I still didn't know what he meant by pawn.

"So, if you do something that doesn't please me, I *will* try to kill you." Nixon was surprisingly helpful, considering that he was trying to destroy his entire race.

Then I noticed the shifting colours in the skin: aqua, navy, cyan, repeating the same pattern over and over. I took it all in. This was real, the war, the blood, the telepathy. All of it.

Aapi let out a wheezing cough and all eyes shifted towards her shadowed shape. She scrunched up her snout in pain as she shifted her position from lying on her side to a more comfortable dog-like posture. She was lucky that Nixon hadn't slashed her airway. If that had happened, she'd be dead.

"Jensen, one more thing. Your father isn't dead."

By the time this registered and I looked back to where he had been standing, Nixon was gone, as if he were a figment of my imagination.

My eyes filled with tears. All this time, all these years, my father had been hiding.

CHAPTER 14

If knowing that my girlfriend's father wanted to kill me every day and that I was the most powerful weapon in the entire universe wasn't bad enough, I had assumed my father died trying to defend his world in the massacre, but no, he'd been hiding all this time, letting me suffer.

The chunk of dirt I sat on by Aapi's head was warm, and the new sunrise beat on my body.

I need to find him. I hadn't gotten any sleep the night before, as this thought had looped around in my head: Despite the bitter life my father sent me, I still loved him. My stubbornness might actually come in handy for once.

Tesla was still sitting in the same gawky position, staring at the glowing coals.

"Tesla, are you—"

"My father showed me things that he thinks are good, but to the rest of the world they are things people only see in their nightmares." She seemed to be squeezing out the information as if it could almost kill her. Sadness clouded her features as she pulled her legs closer to her chest. "Everything's changed, Jensen. I went from being a Wayfinder to being the screwed up, half-blood Rebel everyone hates." She hid her face in her arms and started to sob.

"You're being too hard on yourself." I paused, thinking about what to say. "If it makes you feel better, I have something to do with this situation, too. You were the one who brought me back here."

"To *die*!" she wailed. "Everything you just said only makes me feel worse. I didn't want you, or anyone else in the galaxy, to go through what we are," she said as tears dribbled down her face.

"How were we supposed to know that this was happening? We can still fix it, though, right?" I reassured her. Tesla let out a stuttered breath, trying to calm herself as I brushed some hair out of her lightly freckled face.

She perked up slightly. "If you want to find your father, I have the map," she said, pointing to her wrist.

"I'm not sure if Aapi would be able to make the trek in her condition, I mean, it's asking a lot." Suddenly Aapi heaved herself up off the ground, shaking the snow off her side. And, since I had been leaning on her while we talked, I fell onto my back in the dirt.

"Wow," Tesla stared at Aapi, perplexed.

The cheerful glint in Aapi's eye was comforting. It looked like a river had been painted on her neck from the blue blood that was plastered there, along with pine needles and dirt.

"Will Nixon know where we go?" I asked, hoisting myself onto my feet.

"Phoo, what do you think I am, a beacon? Even if he does take control of me, he wouldn't know where we were unless there was a landmark," she explained.

"Think fast!" she said as she playfully chucked me my helmet. I threw my hands out in front of me to catch it, giving her a small smile.

"That's good. If he could know all, then he would know the Rebels' every move!" I exclaimed, relieved.

"Yeah, then we'd be hooped," Tesla remarked.

I brushed the pine needles out of my insulated helmet before putting it on and throwing open the attached goggle lenses. "So, why doesn't your father try to kill the Rebels from the inside?" I asked.

"Dude! He's not that brainless!" she answered, tossing the gun back down into the snow. "He still loves me . . ." she mumbled.

"One more question. How come you don't need a jacket, or a full shirt?" I continued, lowering my gaze to the ground and tapping my chin.

"Mmm! When have you ever asked this many questions?" Tesla replied. I gave her a you-have-no-idea-what-I've-been-through look, and her face softened.

"I'm still not sure if Aapi should come, though. I know you're the biologist, but I know the terrain," she reflected thoughtfully.

"Good idea, maybe one boring night will do us some good."

Aapi let out a loud snort and I stared at her with a lifted brow. *You obviously don't know the capabilities of telepathy,* Aapi glared back at me. *We share each other's life forces, dummy!* she explained.

Tick . . .

Tick . . .

Just like British Columbia, I thought gloomily as I gazed up at the cloudy, overlayed sky. *Rain isn't the worst thing that could happen. If Tesla and Aapi can handle it, I can at least try,* I reminded myself, turning my gaze to Tesla's small grin.

Also, a big fate dump, if our bond gets stronger, which it will, he will be able to control you too! Aapi explained, sharpening her brows.

So that's why I'm his pawn. You're smart. I rubbed my glowing wrist, agitated by the bitter context.

"So all of our problems… they're because of my father?" I croaked.

"Jensen, your father did something great, but what he did came at a price." Tesla put her hand on my shoulder, touching the glowing cyan protrusions that signified my captainship.

"He may have messed up, but without him, you wouldn't have me, or Aapi," she tried to calm me.

"But he—"

"What? Messed up your life? You were the captain of one of the most advanced ships in the entire galaxy, your family has been honoured many times for what you did for Cacadin. Please respect that, Jen," she finished.

I was speechless. I grabbed her hand as she moved to go back and fix the fire, pulled her to me and gave her a hug, feeling her warm body.

"You're right, Tes. Even after all the things I've been through, I need to respect him." I squeezed her harder. "You are the light of my day and the map that I follow, and even though your father controls you, you still seem to find the bright side to everything!" I gazed into her eyes once more.

CHAPTER 15

I let out a small chuckle as I listened to Tesla's story.

"What about you, Aapi?" I asked, turning the Avigull so the raw side faced the hot fire. The white meat looked and tasted surprisingly like chicken, although it was tougher.

I had insisted that Tesla and Aapi eat some first, but Tesla pointed out that I'd been through the most trauma and used up the most energy in the last few days.

Nothing in my life is exactly worth telling unless you have a strong stomach or a taste for sickening, heartbreaking drama. Aapi flicked her tail, sending melting snow into the air. The rain had slowed to a spitting mist, and we had the fire going properly. Despite Tesla's disinterest in gladiators or drama, she gave a small thumbs up.

"I dissect animals as a job, I think I can handle it," I joked, throwing her a taunting grin.

So help me I will shove your gun down your throat, she thought angrily.

"Oh lighten up, Aapi. Even though you lived through the massacre, you can still joke about it." I poked her in the forearm with my bony elbow and she let out a low growl.

Fine, but don't blame me if you have nightmares for the next month, she thought as she surrendered. Aapi suddenly started to glow a vivid purple as she tilted her head to the sun, and for the first time spoke clear words from her mouth.

"Long ago,
I spoke my true words freely,
prophesy to all who wanted to hear.
And when the day became a reality,
I fought for the only side I knew,
the only side I could be loyal to.
When I fought to protect the ones I taught long ago,
Whenever I fought for my own actions,
I cried out in pain,
I was trapped in a dark hole,
only able to watch them suffer.
And when the sun disappeared and the land was soaked
in blood,
I rose to my feet and fled,
Breaking the chain that kept me linked to my creator.
I fled to the only other family I knew, and when I fell
in love,
And told him everything,
He did not love me . . .
This is my story, do not let your choices be decided
on feelings,
do not trust everything you hear,
The ones you trust will deceive and fall."

I stopped breathing. How could I put her through that?

Aapi took long gasps for air as I tried to piece the whole thing together. I glanced over at Tesla's petrified face, my face, too, painted with fear.

"He tried to wipe out his entire race, Jensen!" she cried out. I was spooked by her hoarse voice as I jumped off the log I was sitting on to grab the now burnt Avigull.

When I speak about the past and future, I use my own words. I am the prophecy of Annoterra, Aapi said, frowning at me while her purple fluorescence disappeared back into her shell. None of our voices broke the silence for at least ten minutes, pure shock flaring in our eyes.

Listen to me, Jensen, a vivid prophecy came to me just before I found you:

Beware the darkness under your noses,
Beware the traitors in your clans.
One will ruin the darkest of plans,
One will bring back the light to our eyes.
When there is an ocean of blood, our planet will be saved,
Although our savior will not make it unscathed.
Find him,
Trust him,
Make the world hopeful again . . .

Aapi, why would you tell me this? Right after your shocking life story?

Our world is yours to protect, from your father and Nixon, she implored.

My eyes were wide with fear, startled by the task at hand.

"Jensen, are you ok?" Tesla asked from the other side of the fire.

"Aapi told me that I have to protect the entire world, and that my victory wouldn't come without some form of scar," I said worriedly.

"Scar, as in . . ." she prompted.

"Emotional, as in me losing something really close to me," I said quietly, throwing Aapi a piece of burnt meat. "Or it could mean that Nixon kills me with my own hands," I rasped, trying to swallow my fear.

I know this might not sound very hero-like, but I don't want to die, I don't want to kill people against my will, or *lose something, or someone, close to me,* I thought quietly.

No one does, Jensen, but at least if we die doing something great, the universe can be light again, Aapi replied calmly. It felt as if she'd changed slightly, from uptight to calm and caring. I passed Tesla the stick with the Avigull on it, staring into the bright white flames of the fire.

"My turn." I changed the subject as my head spun with questions. Still staring into the shifting flames, I thought of a memory to share.

"Ah, now I remember. It was my first day at Cacadin Stratum Two. Man, was I upset. When I found out my mother was going to send me there she'd had to shove me into the ship!" I watched Aapi settle down in the snow again.

"But the moment I stepped off the ship, everything immediately felt better, like nothing could go wrong," I said with gratitude. Tesla looked up from her bird.

"Because I saw you. Zenon bugged me for the next month to go up and talk to you, but I just didn't have the guts to do it." I gave a small shrug, poking the fire with a stick.

"You two changed my life forever. Aapi, mostly because you caught me before I killed myself, and Tesla, because you made my days bright!" They both inched closer to me, settling themselves in the snow.

As long as we are together, as long as none of us die, things won't be so bad. I settled my chin on top of Tesla's head. For once the wind was calm, as if the universe was finally at peace with what I did. The haze was starting to clear, revealing the beautiful mountains. The stony rock face we were settled on was oranges and yellows, reflecting the sun's warm rays. *But if we do die? What would happen then? Does it matter right now? Just enjoy life for once, Jensen. Live life to the fullest, be the thick-skulled Dutch person father always thought you were. Forget the pain of life for once.*

CHAPTER 16

The smouldering fire was the only thing that lit the area. The moon was blocked by dense clouds, and that's all that calmed me enough to get some rest. Even while I slept, thoughts of the massacre looped around in my head, tormenting me. I waited for the sun to rise as I lay with my back toward it in the prickly branches of my makeshift bed. I brushed my long fingers through my knotty hair, then accidentally tickled the new blue skin on my wrist.

Did I leave my sleeve up all night? Gosh I must have been tired. I rolled it back down over my wrist, gazing over at the tall trees as they quivered in the wind.

Jensen, are you awake? Aapi asked quietly from behind me.

Yeah, I didn't get much sleep, I replied tiredly as I rolled over onto my back. I took a deep breath of the scentless air before sitting up in a cross-legged position. Now that I could actually stretch, I cracked my back a few times as I arched it and threw my hands out to the sides.

Hey Jen, you had another dream last night, much more vivid than before, though. You were battling a mirror image of yourself—

I saw it too. It meant that Nixon will try to control me.

It wasn't like that though, he seemed. . . smart. Not like a Nixon-controlled-zombie type thing, she continued.

Visions are weird, we might never know what they mean, I thought as I tried to get a pine needle out of the back of my suit.

Hey Aapi, do I still have blood on my face? I asked as I strained my eyes to look at my nose and failed.

Ha! You look like you spilled something on it! she joked as she stepped over Tesla's relaxed body.

"Ugh." I grabbed a handful of snow and tried to rub the dry crusty blood off my pointy nose. After I had done that I had to scrub my wound, which hurt the most. Like the blue skin on my wrist, it was really sensitive. After all that there was a pile of snow with red flakes in it, and I stood up and booted it as far as I could off the cliff.

"Did I get it all off?" I asked Aapi, who was playing with the coal from the fire, making symbols in one of the remaining pieces of wood.

"What is that?" I asked, pointing to the symbols with my clean hand.

You still have some on your eyebrow, Aapi replied.

"Thanks." I rubbed some more of the dark red blood off my face.

The Annoterran dialect, why? Aapi stated.

"Nixon's coding is almost exactly the same . . . etched imprints, except it's more complex, using dots too." I kicked the log back onto the pile, making sure the writing was face down, which sent a billow of ash into the damp, cold air. Tesla let out a small cough and I started to blush from sympathy. She peered at my damaged face before smiling. I was confused, I hated the long, deep laceration that ruined my friendly look.

"It suits you," she answered quietly as she sat up. "What's Aapi doing?" she asked, pointing to the log that Aapi was writing on again.

"I don't know, journaling?" I shrugged as I bent down and tried to stay upright in a squatting position.

"Makes sense. I would too, but I have to keep everything secret for the sake of Annoterra," she joshed. She put her hand on my back and tried to look me in the eyes but I avoided her. "Is everything ok? Ever since I found you, you seem . . . out of it."

"Maybe, to put it into perspective, Tes, I went from being an honoured pilot to a forsaken Pre-Sighter in a matter of three hours. Plus, got attached to a gladiator monster."

Hey! Aapi shouted, hurt and irritated.

"Ugh!" I hid my face in my hands remorsefully.

"Then we meet, I find out my team is de—" I began.

"Except for Zenon," she interrupted.

"You get what I mean! Also, I find out my father is still alive, of all things. It's just too much to process." I could have carried on but my words had started to come out in a slurry.

"Yeah, hmm, what was it you said?" she tapped her chin. "Ah, fight it as long as you can. Don't give up." She patted my back. Tesla hopped up from her slouched position and kicked some more of the bloody snow off the cliff.

"How do you—"

"My father lets me recall certain things. What a guy, eh?" she said in her rich Canadian accent.

Yeah, typical hero of a father, I thought, rolling my eyes.

I agree, I was raised by him. That stupid smile never left his face, Aapi thought.

Aapi, that wasn't directed to you— Wait, did you just agree with me? I asked, shocked.

That, my friend, means that our bond is getting stronger. I would be excited, but for the well being of our system, I'm really worried. And yes, I did agree with you, she affirmed. I took another short glance at her as she flipped the log back onto the pile.

You shouldn't be so uptight about things, she tried to reason. She stood up and came over to me.

Like me, I'm so grumpy, uptight because of my past! Gaw gaw gaw! she joked in an exaggerated voice, jabbing me in the ribs. I kept my face adamantly straight as she continued to jolt me to the left. I was glad for the thin armour that protected all the vulnerable, thoroughly veined areas.

"I think we should leave," Tesla whispered in a panicked voice. I stood up to see she had my binoculars.

"Hey, where'd y—"

"Run!" she shouted. Tesla suddenly pelted in the other direction, tossing me the binoculars and grabbing my wrist.

Don't you *dare look back! Just keep running!* Aapi screamed, sending a fiery pain through my skull. Tesla let go of my wrist as soon as I caught up to her, still running straight for the cliff that was ahead of us.

"What are you doing?" I asked with a look of panic on my face as she grabbed my wrist again.

"Eject your grappling hook! Quick!" Now I could feel what we were running from as a flurry of snowflakes hit the helmet secured to the shoulder blades of my suit, but what gave it away most was the shudders that came from below my feet: *Avalanche.*

"I still don't—"

"Oh, for Pete's sake!" She grabbed my arm and ejected the small silver hook.

"What about Aapi?"

"She'll be fine, she's done this before!"

Umm . . . I may remind you I was being controlled by Nixon when I did this last! Aapi added. Facing the cloud of snow and rubble she shifted her weight on the trembling ground.

I'm sure you'll be—

Tesla suddenly pushed me over the edge and I let out a yell until my lungs were entirely compressed. We kept falling until my wire ran out and we came to a sudden halt dangling off the edge of the cliff.

"I did not think that through!" Tesla said, clutching my chest.

Laughing, I replied, "You know what, I would have probably done the same." I adjusted my grip on the wire, making sure it wouldn't rip my arm out of its socket. "Except for when you shoved me off the edge of the cliff," I finished.

"You were procrastinating!" Tesla clutched me tighter as the wire quivered under my grip, sending a massive pain down my arm.

It quivered again, this time sharper. It was rubbing against the crag above, causing the line to fray. One of the braided wires gave in and snapped, uncurling from the tight, twisting cord to bend down towards us.

The snow above shifted again, causing another line in the nexus of metal strings to snap.

Chunks of snow tumbled down towards us and I braced myself to get dumped on by a block of powder. A large clump landed square on the crown of my head and I yelped at the freezing cold. "Ack! It's going down my suit!"

"Shhh!" Tesla tried her best not to laugh. "Don't move!"

I whimpered as the clumps of snow slid down to my trap muscles. I stopped fidgeting as another twine abruptly broke. It made the entire line quiver, and now, all four hundred pounds of our weight were tugging on the three remaining wires.

I turned to look down at a dark, deep, freezing cold lake two hundred feet below. That water was more than cold enough to kill somebody like me, who already had low blood pressure. "Oh gosh! No, I don't want to go down there! Definitely not!"

Another wire gave in.

"No! Please, don't let go!" I pleaded.

I can't swim at all. I might slap the water's surface and choke on almost the entire lake, but I couldn't intentionally stay afloat.

Tesla's fingers were dinging into my hips as she slowly slid down my torso. I growled, "Don't you dare let go, Tes!"

"I'm slipping!" She grabbed my waist harder, trying to stop herself from sliding down to my legs. "I might let go. . ." Her fingers loosened their grip. Maybe out of exhaustion, or maybe out of sacrifice. I wouldn't let her sacrifice herself like that. If she was going down, so was I.

Her hands let go entirely and a split second later I grabbed her wrist.

Our weight bobbed against the line and the last wire broke.

We plummeted down to the lake.

She fell in first, disappearing below the surface of the freezing cold freshwater.

The poker straight way I went in sent me more than five feet below the surface. Without a jetpack to take me back to the surface I struggled, reaching up then batting my hands down to try and get back up. I panicked, and that only doubled my air consumption. I swung my head down to look beneath me and all I saw was darkness and the rays of the sun filtering through the water to create a geometric shadow below. I panicked even more as I started to sink, and after a few more kicks my vision started to dissolve.

A distorted voice ringing in my eardrums beckoned, "Jensen!"

Something was shoved down into my chest to flex my sternum and I jolted as the biggest spurt of thick water imaginable came up out of my lungs.

Coughing as the rest of the water came spewing out, I could feel my eyebrows sharpen, tensing.

"Jen!" the voice rang in my ears again.

I squinted up toward the sun in the baby blue sky. "Ugh," I started to sit up and I felt a hand on my back, helping me.

Two of the fingers on that hand started to trace patterns in between my shoulder blades, calming me. Tesla's face greeted me, distressed. "You almost drowned!" Her features turned exasperated, brows furrowing. "I guess I should have taken into consideration that you can't swim, either."

I swallowed, brushing my soggy hair out of my face. "Only one way out—" In the midst of that thought I took a glance around at my surroundings. Soaking wet, freezing cold, and traumatized, I lurched into her, panicked. "How the heck did we get back up here?" I exclaimed, bewildered.

Her lips pursed.

My eyes narrowed, wondering why she had done that so suddenly.

"I. . . uhm. . . jetpacked us back up." Her shoulders tensed slightly and her knuckles whitened.

For a second I didn't believe her. I brushed it off, sniffling as I shivered. "How long was I out?"

"Only a minute or two. Are you okay? Are you cold? Stiff?"

"I'm definitely cold." I pulled my shaky hand up to my face and used the glass pad to turn on the heating system integrated into the suit. I curled my legs into my chest and let out an unsteady breath as steam rose off me. After a few minutes, I rose to my feet.

Staring at the mess of branches, rocks, and brown cement-like snow, I could hardly find where the avalanche started and where it ended. *Nothing I haven't seen before.* Even though I'd seen many avalanches, I still dreaded the thought of thousands of trees getting plowed over.

"We need to find Aapi," I said.

Now that will be a laborious task. First we have to locate her, then dig her out in a pizza-type shape and make sure we are not on top of her, which could cause further damage to her traumatized body. But how could we find her? It's not like Tesla had another one of those Undorian cubes. And Aapi wouldn't be able to tell where we were through that much snow. I wasn't sure how much air Aapi had left or if she was still conscious. Also, what was up with Cacadin not sending us beacons or probes? If we were to go outside and explore under these conditions, shouldn't we have the necessary tools? If not, they may as well send us to death itself.

I started by asking Aapi if she could at least hear what I was thinking about, and again, no answer made our situation even more difficult. Only Aapi knew the full capabilities of telepathic connections, and even if I did, I was somehow already fatigued from the upset in the morning.

"How are we to find her when we can't even remap the area we were camped at?" Tesla asked, throwing one of her hands at the sloughed schute. "I would try to stay calm but that *lobster* was our last defence."

"Tesla! Please don't call her names. I would much rather have her than a pureblood, wouldn't you?" I replied sternly. Tesla gave me an unsure look as I dug my heel into the snow.

"How would you suggest we try to find her?" I changed the subject.

"Well, we should first narrow down the search." She kneeled in the snow, drawing the harsh landscape.

"Judging by where she was when she got buried, and where the cliff ends . . ." She traced the lines over again.

"She would either be under our feet . . ." I added.

"Or over the cliff. Jensen, make a small hole in the ground about two meters ahead of me," she ordered pointing to a small tree lying on top of the snow.

"But wh—"

101

"If you had come to the avalanche safety course, you'd understand. So, as I said, go and make an indent in the ground," she once again interrupted my arguing. I gave a small shrug and estimated two meters over towards the tree. With my steel-toed boot, I carefully etched an indent in the ground, just a little smaller than my hand.

"Now, if I remember correctly, Aapi could be anywhere from that dot to off the cliff." She tapped her chin with the small stick she'd been using to draw with.

"If we first search the north-east side of the cliff we will probably have better luck." She turned towards me as I gazed off in the direction she suggested.

"Why?" I asked slowly.

"Because of the wind direction."

"Right. That's easy, why didn't I think of that?" I asked, kicking a stone across the ground.

"Because you already have enough to worry about," she replied.

"If we were to search, we would need a long pole. I don't suppose a stick would work, would it?"

"Nah, the atoms aren't structurally sound for that, too flexible. But, if we used a different, naturally occurring material . . ."

"What are you suggesting?" I inquired as she looked at me vacantly, thinking.

"I'm not sure if it would work, it's too dangerous," she said apprehensively. "Just tell me what to do. Anything to save another life," I stated confidently. Tesla smiled as I unfolded the glide. "Plus, I've almost killed myself at least five times already,"

I reassured her, handing her one of the small bluetooth earbuds. She put it in her left ear before handing me her gun. I almost dropped it again, but this time I straightened my back to hold the load a little better.

"Also, Jen, you may want to wear your gloves."

"My gloves?" I asked, frightened, feeling the pockets on my legs for a pair of latex gloves. "One problem, after Xomnia, I may or may not have forgotten to restock," I replied sheepishly. Tesla rolled her eyes before handing me a pair of leather gloves. After that, she proceeded to give me a you-were-*not*-prepared look.

"Leather? But mine are latex! What do you expect me to do here?" I panicked.

Tesla rolled her eyes. "Be quick about it," she remarked as she brushed off my comments.

"About what?" I asked while putting my black helmet back on.

"I'll explain while you fly," she sighed.

"How helpful. When you handed me your gun, that's when I started to get worried." I got into position to leap off the cliff, feeling for footholds. I launched off the small rock face just as she started talking to me, testing to see if the earbuds were working.

"Ok Jensen, you're going to have to go find another Kerosene cave."

CHAPTER 17

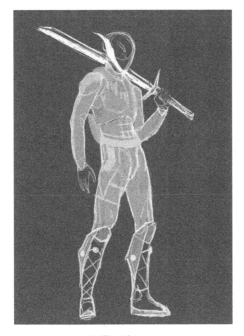

Erillia Claymore

"Tesla! For Pete's sake, woman! Answer me!" I yelled frantically. I rolled to the right as the red-maned cat took a swipe at my head.

"Hurry, Aapi only has a few more minutes!" she reminded loudly as I ducked another fitful swipe.

"What am I looking for again?" I asked impatiently.

"A black, mineral-like water, it drips from the ceiling," Tesla explained. I dodged another pouncing attack and finally had a chance to look around. In the back corner, I saw a blackish-gold liquid with gray flakes dripping into a small pool.

"How am I going to pick it up?" I panicked, trying to shoot the cat in the underbelly.

"Like the mine014; casing on your holster, it shapes into the form of an object. Take some into your hands and think about the object you want to create."

I put Tesla's gun back into my holster and cupped some of the liquid in my hands. It immediately moulded into a lanky Claymore sword with a deep khaki-brown handle, settled into both my hands. I swung the sword to my left, scratching the lion's right forearm and he staggered backward.

I didn't want to injure it too deeply, I was the one invading his territory.

I pointed the sword directly at the cat's chest, warning him that I could strike at any moment, while I crept around him to the entrance. I then lifted back off into the blue sky, not daring to take my eyes off the beast till I was at least a hundred feet away.

A few moments later I landed back on the sloughed wasteland that Aapi was being crushed under.

"Whoa! That's so cool," Tesla breathed as I held the sword up vertically then swung it over to the side.

"For once something actually agrees with me!" I exclaimed proudly. I poured half of it into Tesla's hand and it promptly turned into a long pole. She set her legs apart and stabbed it into the ground until she only had only one or two inches showing. Then I did the same, a shoulder length away. We repeated this for at least three minutes before Tesla finally hit something. My heart leaped as we heard a hollow knocking sound up the pole, signifying that we had finally found her. This time we molded the liquid into wide, square-ended shovels, with me in the back, shoveling away the hardened snow that Tesla picked at.

"How far down do you think she is?" I asked, heaving a big chunk of snow onto my pile.

"Judging by the probe, she's only another few inches away!" she panted, tossing another shovel full of dirty snow at my feet.

I'm just hoping she's alive! I thought, shoveling another solid block behind me. Then, finally, we managed to uncover Aapi's head.

"Oops! I think I poked her in the nose," Tesla gestured at Aapi's bloody snout.

"Oh whatever, at least we found her," I replied, putting two of my fingers on her neck gently, checking for a pulse. "It's faint, but it's there. Tesla, let's finish uncovering her," I said as I reached out to touch Aapi's soft forehead.

"I would have never expected an avalanche with this many trees!" she exclaimed, astonished. She heaved another shovelful over to the pile.

"Wait, Tes, does this area have seasons?" I asked.

"Sort of. It gets a little bit warmer at points in the year, but the snow never melts, so we're stuck with this weird, chalky base layer," she explained as she held up a piece of snow and let it go off in the wind.

"Huh, so then what would trigger it?" I continued.

"Hydras, Avigulls, pretty much anything that can live here. Or it could be triggered by dead trees and snow falling off of a cornice." She sat down beside me in the snow as she tried to slow her breathing.

"So, anything could trigger it?"

"Yes, why?" she asked, throwing some more into the wind. I handed Tesla back her gloves to avoid answering.

If something did trigger that, what would it be? At worst Nixon and a bunch of troops. Or Tesla could be right and it was just—wait, did she say Hydra? My father created a bloodthirsty Hydra of all things!

Aapi let out a cough and our eyes turned to her expectantly.

"She's in bad shape, worse than I thought," I added, rubbing her neck. "What else do you know about treating avalanche trauma?" I quizzed anxiously as Tesla put on her gloves.

"Well, first, you need to make sure she isn't bleeding in any places," she instructed. I checked Aapi's torso as she said this, carefully running my hands on her smooth exoskeleton.

"Then, once she wakes up, you need to ask her what the date is and if she's numb in any areas. I would ask a human if they got snow in any place, but seeing as she was made for this we won't have to worry about that."

When she said *human* my heart skipped a beat. It felt as if I didn't know Tesla very well. Even though she was blue, had glowing blocks scattered on her skin, and didn't get cold in below-zero temperatures, she still acted like the person I'd known a month ago. I still loved her.

"Do we just wait? I'm fine with that, it's not even lunch-time and we've already gotten in an avalanche, fought a lion, and used weird liquid," I joked to relieve the tension. I leaned up against Aapi's chest and let out a small sigh of relief.

"Hehe, you mean the Erillia stone," she giggled. She leaned on Aapi in the same position, laying her head on my shoulder.

"Stone?" I echoed.

"Found in the deepest parts of our cave systems, also one of the very rarest types of rock."

"You just sent me with a five percent chance that I would find that stuff, and a better chance of getting killed? Why would you do that?" I was dumbfounded.

"You said you'd do anything, you heroic maniac." She pulled my chin over so I would look her in the eyes. I gave her a heartfelt smile and a kiss on the cheek.`

"Jensen, why do you still love me, if you're human and I'm—"

"Because you're the sweetest, most wonderful person I know. Who cares what a person looks like? Not me," I admitted. She snuggled up beside me, resting her chin on my shoulder as she let out a sigh.

CHAPTER 18

"**Aapi! Aapi! C'mon, snap out of it,**" I smacked her snout a few times and shone a flashlight in her eyes, checking if her pupils were stable. Her head suddenly popped up and I had to push it back down with all my weight.

Ugh, my head hurts so much, she complained.

Good to hear your voice again, Aapi. I zigzagged the light a few more times before pulling it away.

"She's awake. Should I give her a minute or just fire the questions off?" I asked Tesla, putting my newly molded flashlight back into the chest pocket of my suit.

"Maybe just give her a minute or two to get her bearings," Tesla replied, kneeling by Aapi's head and snapping her fingers together by her ears. They immediately reacted to the sound, lurching away then flicking back to their original position. Her large ears took up most of the space between her jawline and the top of her skull, blocking off the area where her head connected to her long neck.

I can't believe I survived that! Thanks, Jen, she said, staying still in the crystallized snow.

Thanks?

The reason I'm alive is because of your life force.

Well, that would explain why I'm so tired, I rationalized, shifting my crouching position as the snow shuffled under my feet.

"Ok, Aapi, I'm just going to ask you a few questions to check your memory and nerves," I said. "First, do you feel numb anywhere?"

Nope, just my throbbing head. She shifted her gawky posture.

"Ok, second, what is the date? Start with the day."

I bet you don't even know that, she rassed.

Aapi, just answer the question, I replied gravely.

Sigh . . . Wednesday, May ninth, twenty-one sixty-three.

"Hey Tes, is it Wednesday?" I asked quietly. Tesla gave me a are-you-kidding-me look, crossing her arms.

"You're fine. Just rest," I reassured Aapi, standing up and going over to Tesla.

"Tesla, umm . . . I've been thinking about this for a while and," I paused, scratching my head and avoiding her gaze. "I should go on to find my father alone. I can't risk almost killing you guys again."

"But without Aapi, you—"

"It's not worth it, Tes. I've already decided," I stated resignedly. I swept past her to grab my gun, which I had removed to take the weight off of my body as I shoveled the snow, when she grabbed my hand.

"Tesla, please," I croaked, still staring at the gun to avoid her face. "My family problems are bigger than you can even think to imagine." I held back my tears. "If I lost you or Aapi, that's it . . . I would probably kill myself." My throat seized up with pain from the tears I was now desperately holding back. I couldn't look her in the eyes if I tried.

"Just . . . don't kill yourself, if you're going to go alone," she said affectionally. I turned around and gave her a big hug.

"I just can't lose you. I've lost you once, not ever again," I said firmly.

She probably wouldn't understand what it meant to me, for someone to let me go on my own, and not hold me back, to let me fix my mistakes, voice my opinion. Then, letting go of her slowly, I turned from her kind face, grabbed my gun and helmet, and started towards the dense forest.

"Jensen, wait!" Her words stopped me this time. I turned back to her as she grabbed a paper and pen from her belt.

"If you're going to find your father, you need a map. Here." She handed me a small piece of paper and headed back over towards Aapi's relaxed body. I put my helmet back on gently as I gazed at her light sketch. The only thing I was glad about the map was her writing. It was human and it was neat. Could I leave them? Would that be fair? This was important to me, but if I left Tesla to help Aapi, when Aapi was my responsibility . . . Tesla wasn't strong or thick-skulled like I was. She was innocent and kind. I quickly looked back at her, just for safe measure, to see her sitting down against Aapi, lying her head on Aapi's to keep her calm.

Go find your father, Aapi thought supportively.

Thanks Aapi.

After a few minutes I could no longer see them as I disappeared through the prickly spruce.

CHAPTER 19

My heart was pounding out of my chest as I ran on the treacherous cornice for my life, making the powdery unstable snow tumble down the mountain to its death . . . metaphorically speaking. The map Tesla drew for me failed to do its job. The entire rock face I was supposed to walk along slid away down the side of the mountain and I was pushed to the top of this nightmare. The creatures chasing me were no doubt Acolite, but the way they trudged through the snow, the way they carried their weapons, it was almost as if they wanted to be spotted. It didn't seem logical for them to be Rebels, although they were not robots like the ones that shot me in the tower. It was confusing, but if I pushed it out of my mind I would never know.

And if it was the Rebels, would they kill me? Nixon wouldn't, unless I stopped the war, or stole back all the Acolites. So in other words, are the Rebels on Annoterra different than Rebels on Earth? If they are, what would they be like, and why would they make so much noise? Am I sticking my neck out for people who have a death wish? My gut hurt, I felt like throwing up, but like any stubborn man I kept pelting towards the many peaks that stood still, waiting for me. Even with my fast pace, it seemed as if I wasn't running at all. The wide expanse visible on this non-polluted world made it seem fifty times bigger than Earth.

The cornice ahead had slid away into an avalanche, then reappeared about a meter further on.

Gonna have to jump for it! I should be able to make that, right?

The gap came closer with every breath, making me question my intention numerous times. I knew for sure it was the right decision when I was in sight of the Acolites and they started to shoot at me vehemently.

I leapt for the other side with all my remaining strength. Thankfully the snow held underneath my feet, giving me extra leverage. But even with that I didn't make it all the way across and clung desperately to the ledge. The impact knocked the breath out of my broad chest and for a second I thought I had collapsed my lungs. I inhaled sharply, trying to regain control of my breathing. The high thin air did not give much oxygen worth spending.

I'm probably going to die. Well, it was fun, went through pain, rescued my girlfriend from her own father, found out that my father was alive, and got attached to a crayfish. Decent way to spend a miserable life.

"Get him out of there," a gravelly voice ordered just before I felt strong hands grip my arms. I kept my head low as they flung me down on the coarse snow and threw my helmet off. I sat up on my knees, still glaring at the sand-like ground.

"You're an interesting fellow, aren't you?" He grabbed my face and I was forced to look him in the eyes, squinting against the bright sun. He had dark green eyes, reflecting his semi-transparent navy blue skin.

"Now, what would you be doing on Annoterra?" he asked. I jerked away from his hand, returning my gaze to the ground.

"I . . . crashed," I replied. I felt two more Acolites tie my hands behind my back. I had a sudden flashback of the flying pieces of metal and glass. The vibrant coloured system hadn't even come close to soothing my pain.

"Why don't you tell me who you really are? I'll trust you're a pilot, but you're way too tall to be a normal human."

"I'm not saying a word about myself," I replied as I tried to slip free of the thick ropes.

"You've got a temper. Bring him back to camp," he ordered a mint-coloured woman. She suddenly lifted me over her shoulder, her pointy collarbone digging into my stomach. Then I noticed why she could carry me so effort-lessly: the added metal backbone structure and leg attach-ments. Her legs were shaped like Aapi's: down, back, down, forward and then the wide foot.

The ride was excruciating. The up and down motion was almost worse than my aching gut, sending a sharp pain through my chest. I'm not the most flexible person in the world either, so the woman was stuck carrying a log more than a body. If that wasn't bad enough, the tall woman shook snow off the trees, sending flurries down my back.

"Rebel, eh?" I questioned. She didn't answer, her glass-like ears just twitched slightly towards the sound. I could now see the large fire blowing in the wind through the trees, making the air smokey and hard to inhale. There, around the fire, sat a few more Acolites: blue, purple, indigo, and another shorter, grayish-coloured one that sat slouched in the wet snow.

Why does everyone chuck me in the snow, on my back? That's literally what she did, leaving me far away from the fire.

"Back so soon?" the indigo woman joshed in a silky tone.

"That alien may have just saved me an extra five mile hike." She sat down beside the other woman on the log, stretching her mechanical counterparts out to reach the fire.

"What is it doing here?" The blue one stared at me coldly. The mint Acolite shrugged, putting all her upper weight on her knees.

"All it said is that it crashed. Dr. Martezz somehow trusts that he is a pilot. Although, I haven't seen any debris *or* crashed ships in the northern parts," she said. She glowered at me nastily. By the time the safeguard returned to the garrison, my shoulders felt like they might fall off from the constant numb pain that shot up my back into my neck. The small white tents on the outer rim of the camp distorted my view of the sharp cliff that I had almost fallen off of.

The technology I had experienced so far clouded my thoughts with worry about the tortures they might use to get false truths out of me. Their tech was already as good or better than ours. Nixon had the ability to implant Acolites into computers with the Google platform, then use them in arsenals of highly weaponized robots with the aim of a hawk. And their ships were beyond what I could have imagined from such a young planet. Unlike Earth's many formats, they take their animals and combine the abilities of at least five different apex predators into a war machine capable of destroying the Kuiper Belt.

"Where's the human, Zara?" Martezz barked at the mint Acolite that had carried me as he burst heavily into the camp. He glared at her, his thick pants swaying in the wind. She skittishly pointed to me with her strong fingers and went back to staring into the bright orange flames. I crawled back as best I could as he came uncomfortably close to me, inspecting me tediously with his inquisitive eyes. What bugged me most was how long he stared at my damaged face. I knew the burnt skin wasn't the most attractive and was very predominant, but did he have to be rude? After a few moments he sat down in the snow across from me, casting a long shadow as the sun went down again on the horizon.

"So, I won't ask any hard questions, but may I know your name to begin with?" he asked.

"I'm surprised," I commented blankly.

"How so?" He rested his chin on his knuckles.

"Well, that you're coming out this non-threatening. I thought you'd be like N—" I cut myself off, remembering that he was a Rebel and would interrogate me even further to the point of torture.

He raised his brow gently. "Carry on."

"Umm, you wanted to know my name?"

"Yes, that would be very helpful." He scratched his bald head lightly, pulsing the pressure points to a darker blue.

"I'm Jensen Keaton Galantis." All eyes turned towards me. "Captain and biologist of the recently destroyed *Annex*. Our dreadnaught was destroyed by Nixon's battleships and

I have been surviving out in this dangerous forest for four days now." Martezz continued to stare at me, his stone-like face not changing its expression even a little to accommodate the interesting news.

"Unfortunate. Here is another, hopefully less disturbing question. Why are you so tall? I don't mean to be rude, but it's rather intriguing how you've come to be this tall." This had to be the most irritating question in my entire life. Everyone seemed to ask that.

"If you untie me, I can answer all your questions." I lifted my gaze to his shadowed figure. He had a vest, red and slick, with a few small pockets on the bottom and on his chest. His pants were a flexible black jean-like material, connecting to his flat, tall boots.

"How can I be sure I can trust you? How do I know you won't slaughter us and bring our bodies back to Earth?" He leaned in closer to me, almost whispering.

"I can tell you, we do not kill other races for examination," I said quietly. "How can I persuade . . ."

The only way, without telling them anything about Aapi, is to tell them about my father. "I'm the son of Keaton Psalm Galantis, creator of the dirt we stand on."

He immediately released me, putting up two fingers to call Zara over to untie my wrists with another flaming blade like Tesla's. She ran back to the fire quickly and dropped it in before the small flame was able to reach her hands. I rubbed my wrists stiffly, holding my gaze to the snow.

"Thanks."

I rolled up my suit to reveal the now navy blue skin, and his face turned white with fear and astonishment as he grabbed my hand, yanking me forward almost into his lap. He rubbed one of the marks back and forth with his rough hands to reveal a livid darker blue. After that, not even loosening his grip, he reached into the chest pocket of his vest and pulled out a flashlight-like metal case.

"Worst fear?"

"P-pardon?" I stuttered.

"I need to know your worst fear. Everyone has one," he said calmly, inspecting the marks further.

"Hmm . . . dying, Nixon killing my only remaining family members, being used against my will to take innocent lives. Gosh, I hope that never happens." His question was disturbing, but clear. I'd thought about these fears almost every day and dreaded the fifty-fifty chance they could happen, even though I'd been doing everything in my power to make sure they did not become reality. It still seemed to come close every time.

He then lifted the metal case up to my neck and pushed a small needle into my artery. I suddenly felt odd and my vision of the outside world disappeared, sending a chill down my spine. I felt myself in a warm field, the sun beating on my body with its rays, heating my cool face.

What did Martezz do to me? Is this a dream? If it is, why can I feel the sun's warm rays? If this is a dream, why can I control my body? I looked around cautiously at the tall grass, shifting my grip on my sword as I poked cautiously for snakes and coyotes. When I looked down, I noticed I was wearing navy jeans and a green long-sleeved top with a light, unzipped vest and gray runners.

I hadn't worn jeans in so long, I had started to forget how stiff and durable they were.

The sounds of the swaying grass and the strong wind were interrupted by a gunshot, which sent a delayed chill down my spine as I thought about the many scenarios that could have been going on: hunting, war, combat, quarrels among enemies? All of a sudden it didn't matter. Another one of the large white masses shot past my head and hit a tall man standing about a hundred feet away. I whipped toward the sound, fingers gripping the leather hilt of my sword, to face the person as he dropped to the ground, smoke sizzling from his chest with a revolting burnt smell. My eyes traced the daunting broad shoulders, long torso, and the familiar jut of the chin. Something in me was starting to crack. I felt my hand muscles tighten around the leather-handled sword as if I wasn't in control of my body anymore. His now pale skin was almost a complement to the bright yellow grass that stirred at my feet. I took in all of his intimidating features like a lightning bolt. My gaze hit the gaping hole in his broad chest and my eyes filled with warm tears as I realized who it was. My brother.

The brother I'd lost so many years ago, dead yet again, motionless in front of me.

Why would he be here? He died! I spun back around furiously, holding up my long sword.

"Nixon!" I shouted at the swaying field. "Come out and fight me! We can end this here and now!" He suddenly appeared in the distance, his wide gladius sword in one hand pointed at the ground as he walked toward me with a small, pompous smile. He stopped about ten feet away and gazed down at my brother's scorched body.

"This has gone too far!" I shouted. He kept his gaze on the lifeless body.

"I would have liked you to throw an axe at me or something. You're all bark and no bite," he replied, stabbing his sword into the dark soil and crossing his arms.

"You would have caught it and thrown it back," I shrugged. "As far as I understand, in this messed up world my brother died on a space mission with my father, fourteen years ago. He got crushed under a bunch of rocks." I kept my cold glare on Nixon. He moved sideways a few steps away from the body as he got a whiff of the potent stench that I had been unwillingly breathing in.

"This is what *will* happen Jensen. If you don't want this to happen in reality, you'd better fix your attitude and gather the information about what really happened to your father's planet and your family." He pointed at me with one of his long fingers. I launched myself at him and he ducked out of the way. I forced an angry yell as I swung my sword to the left and had to stagger after it to counteract the weight. He let out a deranged chuckle and I felt Tesla's eerie presence.

"Let her go, Nixon!" I leapt at him again and swung my sword to the right, just missing his sturdy torso and sending a bunch of tall grass flying into the wind.

Now I had two problems: Nixon's extreme strength and combat abilities, and the electric discs Tesla was slashing at me. I staggered backward again, tripping over a log that was haphazardly strewn across the ground.

"I didn't want to kill your brother, Jensen. But he kept getting under my skin, so I had no choice but to stop him," he confessed through Tesla's slender body, leaning over me. I crawled backwards quickly, stood up and pointed my long silver blade at him.

It's just a dream! I'm a Pre-Sighter, it's probably mixed in! This thought didn't calm me or convince me. The wind stung my face and I was being cornered towards a cliff. Tesla threw one of her sharp discs to hit me in the shoulder, sending a shallow cut into my arm.

"Stand and fight me, Jensen! Don't cower like last time I cut your face!" he shouted, spinning his sword in one hand. I suddenly spun around and jumped off the cliff, turning my sword into a grappling hook to swing me back up and around behind Nixon. I turned the grappling hook back into my sword, pointing it at him. I thought I had the upper hand when Tesla suddenly kicked me over into the rich black soil. I flipped as she attacked, kicking her in the stomach while she tried to drive her discs into my chest, but that didn't shake her off. She kept holding on to my wide shoulders and I used all of my strength to keep her away from me. I managed to flip the situation, getting on top of her and avoiding her kicks and slices from her blades.

"Tesla, please! C'mon, you can fight him!" I encouraged her. Just as her eyes started to flicker, I put my hand on her cheek.

"Jensen! Help me!" she cried quietly as her eyes seemed to disappear into black holes.

"It's not worth it! Let her go. She gets more bloodthirsty by the second, and there is nothing you can do about it!"

Nixon shouted from behind me. I leapt up and threw my sword at him, turning it into a bunch of tiny daggers. He jumped to avoid them and shot them all back at me. I caught my breath and tried to dodge as they came firing back, but two hit me in the chest and sent a spiky pain through my body.

All I knew after that was the unbearable pain that came with my mistake.

I gasped for air as I returned to consciousness, although the fiery pain was still there, this time from my wrist to my chest, almost stopping my breathing.

"What's going on? What on Earth did you do to me?" I glared down at my arm to see veins popping out and my skin a blistering red. My hand shook vigorously as I put it out in front of my face. I couldn't move my arm, it was either seized up from the swelling and searing pain or its nerves were shot.

"Hmm . . . I didn't expect this. Sit still, Jensen," Martezz commanded. He leaned over and grabbed some snow, which sizzled as he put it on my arm as if I were a barbeque that had caught on fire from too much grease. I moved around uncomfortably as the pain shot further into my chest, taking my lungs hostage and almost stopping my breathing again.

"Sit still? Martezz, I feel like I'm going into anaphylactic shock and you want me to sit still?" I grasped my neck with my free hand as the pain went up into my jaw. I let out a shout of frustration and agony as I felt an extreme headache and dizziness hit me suddenly.

"Take his shirt off, quickly," he summoned two Acolites to come and unzip my shell and take off my shirt to reveal dark blue veins popping out of my chest and back. He then drenched me in snow, which didn't dull the pain or the blazing hot temperature readings Martezz was getting.

"I've never seen such a reaction. Mind you, I've never had a human go through this transformation before," he marveled.

"What. About. Tesla Axis?" I forced out, trying to calm myself.

"Lieutenant Axis was born with Acolite blood. Her markings came through a rash and her skin changed colour and consistency over time." He stabbed another needle into my neck, which soothed the pain slightly. "How did you come to know about her, anyway?" he asked..

I rubbed my sore neck as it cooled off somewhat from the anesthetic. "She was my Wayfinder." Another wave of pain came from my arm. I took a sharp breath and grasped my forearm. He smacked my hand and I had to let go.

"Don't try to stop it."

"Do you want me to pass out?" I asked, as he got up and headed towards one of the tents.

"If you try to stop it, it won't finish the process. Just lie down in the snow and relax. I'll be back in a few minutes to check on you." He looked at me sternly before stepping into the tent.

CHAPTER 20

I didn't get any rest, the persistent pounding in my skull not giving me any relief from the pain or from the emotions of what had happened earlier.

Martezz returned shortly with a notepad and pen, writing down my temperature and pulse every five minutes or so. The entire night he sat beside me quietly, taking notes and drenching me in more snow and giving me water, doing the best he could with the materials he had.

He told me that when Nixon attacked the Rebel base, he had lost all his advanced medical equipment and research.

He also asked me to stop calling them Acolites. They were called Bucromians Acolites, and because their given names had similar meanings, they stuck with the culture name.

"Martezz," I prompted, as he sat back down beside me on a piece of wood.

"Hmm?"

"Will I go through the same transformation as Tesla?" I took in another sharp breath as more heat came from my arm.

"I'm not entirely sure. Judging by the blood samples I've taken you will not, though I am also not sure why whoever-you-root-for would even bother putting you through this pain for warmer blood if you have been fine all this time," he said quizzically. I gave him a you-can-share-your-opinion look as he took another heart rate reading, pushing a sphere up to my neck for a few seconds, then writing down the number.

"Maybe the universe thought it would be easier for you if you could go without all that thick material around your body." He put the pen up to his cheek and turned his gaze to my swollen, numb arm.

"Huh." He poked my arm and I winced. "Still hurts?" I nodded disappointedly.

"As long as you don't mind me asking, what are those things in your ears?" He reached out to grab one with his thick hand and I smacked it.

"Earbuds. They let me listen to music," I said defensively. He raised a brow slightly.

"You mean you can listen to music digitally? Whoa, news to me. What would they be connected to?" he asked, intrigued. I pried the earbud away from my ear, handing the silver object to him. He examined it closely, as if it were a new species of parasite.

"I have a biology tablet, that's where I store them, it's a closed circuit so Ca— so my company couldn't find them." He continued to examine the earpiece, peering at all the rubber fittings, volume buttons, mute button, reset holes and speakers, almost touching it with his nose.

My father didn't even create earbuds? Wow, guess he was either going off grid or thought they were useless.

"You wouldn't have happened to bring back my helmet, would you?" I asked. He handed me the earbud and lowered his vision to the less distracting objects around him so he could think, then turned his gaze back to me.

"Hmm, I think so. If we did it would be in Crosby's tent." He tapped his black pen on his chin. "I do not suggest you go in there, though," he added.

"Why?" I asked.

"He tends to be very suspicious and jumps to conclusions. I'd better do it." He heaved himself off the piece of timber, heading towards the ring of tents. When he returned with my helmet I was relieved to see it was not scuffed or dented any worse than it already had been.

"Thanks, Martezz," I said, relieved. I set my helmet down in the snow.

"No problem. You don't have to call me Martezz, though."

"What should I call you, then?" This time I felt the hot spiny pain go down my left leg and I clutched it, just before I remembered what he told me last time.

"Walker," he replied. I shook his hand with my less numb arm. "What did you do before you were a pilot and a biologist?" he asked. It caught me off guard. My memories came back to me and I lowered my gaze to the ground.

"That's all I've ever been." My eyes were clouded with pain as I unsnapped the dials on my boots. He inspected me, sympathy flooding his features. "What about you?" I asked.

"Before the war started I was an inventor. But afterward I just couldn't bring myself to look at another weapon of any size." He looked unsettled now.

"Yeah, I know what you mean. All this time I thought my family were dead, except for my mother, and now, neither my brother nor father is dead."

"But isn't that a good thing?"

"Not in my world. My father took my childhood away from me and my brother took my love for spaceships and father along with him," I said resentfully. I shifted my position in the snow.

"Your blood sugar seems to be low. I'll go and grab you something to eat."

"Thanks again . . . Walker."

After about ten minutes he returned with a white fruit, which looked like a snowball with blue lines through it.

"What is this?" I took the fruit with my good hand, which wasn't as numb as before.

"It's a Kasaid. Unlike most of the other fruits in the region it tastes like water and has an amazing amount of natural sugar," he explained.

"How do I—" I began and he handed me a small knife as an answer. I started to cut the fruit carefully like a watermelon, holding it in my strong hand and resting the knife in the other, making sure I didn't get any of the juice on my suit. Walker continued to take notes as I ate the tasteless fruit, which surprisingly brought my energy level up and kept the heat down more than the anethstetic.

"How long has the war been going on?" I asked as I grabbed another one of the cantaloupe-like slices.

"Ten years," he said. I almost spit out my food at the thought of being in a war for that long.

"I should have been here sooner!" I finished the last slice and chucked the peels into the bush.

"Why?" Walker asked cautiously, closing his notebook.

"So that I can stop this stupid thing! I can't let you guys suffer any longer." I tried to stand up and found the nerves in my legs were shot. "I can't believe I will probably have to kill my girlfriend's dad. Gosh, I can't do that, for the sake of her well-being." I rubbed the back of my neck.

"Lieutenant Axis is your girlfriend?" he asked.

I couldn't help thinking about her kind face, I missed her so much.

"Well, I suppose I can tell, seeing as you know all my secrets," I mumbled, thinking how lucky I was to have a person like Tesla. "After our friend got caught in an avalanche, I decided to leave them to find my father. It seemed like the right time to me. She didn't want me to leave, but she loves me so she let me go." I struggled to hold back my tears, although I was certain Walker could see my pain. "I don't know . . . ever since this whole thing started, my judgement has been clouded and most of the time it has ended up with somebody almost getting killed." I rested my chin on my knuckles and poked my other hand into the snow with more sizzling noises.

"I see. Don't worry, Jensen, we all feel the same sometimes," he said. I thought I would never hear such a smooth voice from him, his expression changed into a more relaxed, comfortable posture. "But we have to use our best judgment based on what we know at the moment."

"That thing you gave me. The one that gave me the hyper-realistic dream. Nixon said the same, sort of."

"Nixon? Why, what did he say?" He grabbed his notebook again.

"He said that in order to make it through this mess I have to fix my attitude and find out what really happened to my family. Why on Earth would he help me?"

He finished writing his notes. "I think your Pre-Sighter side predicted the future and gave you advice through him. It wasn't actually Nixon in your dream."

"Huh. So my brother *will* die," I said uncertainly. I tried to brush my knotty bagel cut back with my shaky fingers.

"No, he will die unless you can stop this in time." He gestured to the tents and battle-ready Bucromians.

So, you're telling me I have to stop thirty-year-old Bucromians, save my brother, and find my father? You've got to be kidding me.

"But I'm just a biologist! How could I kill anyone? I mean, if you saw me with a sword you would probably barf." My excuses were useless. It seemed that the way things were going, I had been waiting for this my entire life. So why not spend the rest of my life helping these people?

"If you really are the Pre-Sighter, your body will react the way it's supposed to. Whoever controls our universe, they chose you." He wrote a few more notes, paused to think, then wrote a little bit more. "Do you need anything else before I bring the team on another safeguard?" he asked.

"No. But please, if you see Te— Lieutenant Axis, don't shoot her." He grinned reassuringly, then got up from his cedar log, gathered a small portion of the group, and headed back into the trees along the packed path.

CHAPTER 21

When they returned without Tesla or Aapi my heart sank. I longed to hear their voices and see their faces again. The rest of the day was clouded with the worry that they got attacked again or caught in another avalanche. By this time I was able to move around the camp, stretching my numb legs and answering the many questions they had for me:

"Why are you so tall?"

"Why do you have hair on your head?"

"Where did you get such a deep scar?"

"What was it like rescuing someone from an avalanche?"

"How many days have you been living out here?"

They sounded more like children than furious warriors as they poked and prodded me curiously. I had many questions for them, too, but I didn't feel it was the appropriate time or place. I was their guest, so it was only fair for them to ask questions about my looks and recent adventures or mishaps. They insisted on hearing everything in extreme detail from start to finish, which took up most of the evening, and they insisted I continue on in the morning.

And so I did. I resumed from where we got blown into pieces in space. They wanted to hear my entire life's experiences, from when I was two to twenty-one. While I was talking, Walker wanted me to eat another one of the Kasaid fruits.

"Why do I need to eat another?" I asked as he handed me the fruit.

"You're a biologist, right? How else do mammals get their sugar?" I glared at the ground as I realized the easily fixable problem.

"Fine." Why would I even try to argue with a doctor? Maybe it was just the painful and tired state I was in. I took the fruit and fetched the small knife from where I had left it by my shirt.

"After I told Lieutenant Axis I was the Pre-Sighter," I continued, "her father started to control her. Then she tried to shoot me with her huge gun, but she ended up shooting the Avigull eggs that I had left on the rock shelf." I grabbed another small piece of fruit as they burst out laughing.

"Then I had to pin her to the floor and tell my friend to run, which turned out to be a bad idea, because that's how I got this scar. She swiped her flaming blade at me and hit me across the face." I pointed to the long wound that ran from my nose to just above my collarbone.

"Whoa! If I had that happen to me I would be all like: Oh no, my beautiful face! Just take my life!" The indigo Bucromian dropped to the ground and clutched her face, sending snow into the air. I let out a loud laugh, and helped her back up. With their mechanical legs they were even taller than me, making me feel a little more comfortable. It always seemed easier when I didn't have to look down at someone.

"And yet, you guys aren't giving up, even after times started getting tough," I complimented, tossing the peels into the fire.

"Yeah, if we tried, the council would stop us," the blue one added.

"Carry on. I want to hear what happens next!" Zara demanded playfully. I smiled, then paused to think.

"Ok, so then I tied her up with my grappling hook! So Nixon was all like: No! You've won this time, Pre-Sighter!" I exclaimed dramatically. I extended my grappling hook around Zara, who also went tumbling to the ground, flailing her legs. They all burst out laughing again as I tried to wind my wire back up without having to put my suit back on entirely. She hopped back up, dusting off her pants.

"After that, we had to find our friend," I concluded.

"Oh yeah, who is this person? We haven't heard much about her," the blue one observed.

"Well—" Suddenly something landed on top of me, knocking me over into the snow.

"Tesla!" I shouted, pulling her into a hug. She hugged me as tight as she could, squeezing the breath out of my chest.

"Aaa! Can't breathe!" I warned, trying to inhale.

"I was so worried! When I saw the rockslide I thought you g— why are you so warm?" She released me from her grip and glared down at my deep chest.

I took in a deep breath, raised a finger, and said, "Before I answer that, where is Aapi?" Tesla stood up and pulled me up after, still taking sideways glances at my navy chest.

"She's over by the cor—"

135

"What?" I knew what she was about to say, and a shudder of fear ran through my body. I ran as fast as I could out of the camp towards the cliff. I heard Aapi's snarl and stopped on the ledge, just above Walker, who was standing on top of Aapi.

"Walker! Stop!" I shouted furiously as he was about to drive his sword into her chest. He suddenly lifted his sword away from Aapi and glared at me.

"Let me take care of this, Jensen! You don't understand what she's done to us!"

"I know perfectly well what she's done, Walker. You don't understand, she's changed. She wants to help!"

He returned his sword back to his back, still glaring daggers at Aapi.

Are you ok?

I'm fine, she answered. She came over to me, licking me on the side of the face. She peered at my chest too, and I gave her an everything-is-fine look.

"Here is another question, if you're ready for it," Tesla prepared me.

"Fire it off," I said, resigned. She poked my shoulder, sending a dull pain up my neck.

"What's up with your skin?" she asked.

I was surprised to find, as I looked down at my skin, a crystal-like surface.

"What the?"

"I think we better sit down and talk." She grabbed my hand tightly and I had to follow her back to the fire at the camp. She started to list off her worrying questions.

"What's going on with you, Jensen? As soon as I get here, I see you shirtless and hot as a blazing, well, fire," her words rushed out, and then her shoulders went limp.

I sat down on the snow-covered log beside her with more sizzling noises. "Walker made me have a reaction to the markings on my wrist." I pointed to my glowing aqua symbols. "So the entire time you haven't been here, I've been sitting in the snow and eating tasteless fruit," I joked, throwing my hands up in the air and then smacking them back on my knees painfully. I winced as she poked me in the arm, seized back, then put her hand on my back.

"So, what is all this?" She gestured to my navy, lined torso. Suddenly Walker walked up and pushed another needle into my neck, extracting some of the blue blood. She glared at it, horrified, as he handed it to her carefully.

He can't just randomly take my blood. I have something called personal space! I rolled my head, rubbing the sore artery in my neck as I grimaced slightly.

"I believe, Lieutenant, his blood has now changed its genetic structure and his skin is carrying a dangerously high amount of boron nitride, reforming the molecular structure of the skin into a hexagon," he said. I hid my smile in one of my large hands, his subtlety was almost too comical. "To him it's not dangerous, but to any other human it's fatal," he concluded.

She stared at me worriedly. "What does that mean? How is his body reacting to it in a remotely good way? He's still human . . . " She had a mortified look. "Right?" She gazed at Walker and then back at me.

137

"His body carries the nitrogen for boron nitride, and I suppose—"

"Nixon did this, he gave me fluids to keep me alive when I was unconscious, and Aa— our friend said I was his pawn," I pieced it all together as Tesla scowled at me in pure shock.

"Sounds like him." She went back to look at my blood sample. "How is he not, you know, burning up?" she asked.

"The reaction did start with minor burning, but as you may know from Titus, wurtzite boron nitride is the most heat-resistant rock in the known galaxy, so really, you could throw him into this fire and he would be fine." He rubbed my other shoulder with his thumb, ignoring Tesla's pale face. He chuckled quietly in his gravelly tone. "Except for his clothes, of course, they would melt in a matter of seconds."

"As long as he isn't burning from the inside out, I trust you. Thank you for not killing him," she said gratefully.

"You're welcome." He headed back into the woods, carrying his small bag on his shoulder.

"Oh, one more question," I called. He turned on his heel slowly to gaze at me. "Will all this—" I gestured to the shiny coating on my pale skin "—fade after a while?"

He gave a little snort, a smile on his face. "That's for you to find out." He continued into the bush.

"Great," I grumbled.

Aapi collapsed on the ground by the fire with a large thud, warming her wide reptilian feet.

Well, don't you look pretty, Aapi teased.

Haha, very funny.

No, I'm serious, your skin looks like it has ice crystals hardened in it, Aapi stated. I rubbed her head as she settled it on her forearms.

"So, did you guys have a little adventure too?"

"Oh yeah. The first night after you left we got attacked by wolves," Tesla said. My head jerked up and I gaped at her with a horrified are-you-ok expression.

"What? You're allowed to go get yourself killed and I have to say zit, zilch, zero about my mishaps? Trust me, I was fine handling it on my own." She put her hand on my arm and lurched back as if she almost burned herself. "Why are you this hot?"

"Depends on what you mean." She smacked me on the back of the shoulder as I smiled at her mischievously.

"I mean, your skin is almost burning. I can't imagine how painful that must be," she said.

"It feels like I've been running for a week straight then dropped onto a bed of thorns." I think she was a little shocked I even answered. Her expression was a mixture of horror and sympathy.

"Ouch, I'm surprised you didn't just go jump in the freezing river." She gazed over at the large waterway that ran right by the camp.

"Until now I couldn't, I was paralyzed from the waist down." That freaked her out even more and she poked my leg to see if I would react.

"Tesla, my legs are fine. Please just forget this ever happened." I looked her in the eyes and she avoided mine.

"I can't." She brushed some silvery hair out of her face. "The harder I try, the more it comes back. And now I can't even touch you!" She buried her face in her hands, turning her gaze to the ground as a tear fell down one of her pale cheeks. I put one of my large hands on her back, just before I realized that would probably make her more uncomfortable.

"Tesla? I . . ." I started to cry quietly, closing my eyes and trying to blink the tears away.

Why are you crying, Jensen? Aapi asked.

All I want her to know is that I love her and that I will protect her with my life. But I can't even choke it out!

Even when I heard Aapi writing on a log I didn't open my eyes, I was drowning in my thoughts. *Maybe I should just run away in the night so she won't follow.*

Tesla stopped crying and glanced up, rubbing her wet face.

Don't worry, Jen, everything will be ok, Aapi encouraged.

I rubbed one of my tears away with the edge of my palm. *Why?*

Because if we stick together, we can achieve the impossible. And my only wish is to see you two happy. My purpose is to make sure you don't do anything stupid, but that means you have to get up again. Heroes are allowed to cry, but they have to learn to get back up, Aapi continued.

I suddenly felt Tesla's cool body on mine, her stuttered breathing warming my heart. I hugged her back, holding her in my arms.

"What did she write on the log?" I asked.

"She said that you wanted to tell me: You taught me how to be brave and to fight for what I love and believe in. Without you I'd be a lost fool," Tesla interpreted.

It was true, I loved her like the stars in the sky. She loosened her grip slightly to look at me, her purple eyes highlighting her pastel mint skin.

"Nothing can stop me from loving you, Jensen. I trust you with my life. Getting mildly burned by your touch is worth the risk," she reassured me. I wiped away another of her small tears as it tried to make it out of her animated eyes, forgetting about my surroundings, lost in her deep gaze.

"Well, that's good, maybe now we can stay together. Can I go dunk myself in a river now?" She let out a sweet giggle before nodding.

CHAPTER 22

I felt the freezing water rush over me as I dunked myself in the strong current, relieved as the pain loosened its hold on my chest so I could breathe freely again. Tesla suddenly burst out laughing. I quickly realized why and tried to bat the thick steam away from my face as it clouded my vision of the shoreline.

"Feel better, steamy?" she joshed, cupping some of the clear water from the broad, white-water river in her hand and taking a drink. Her thick braid slipped out of her other hand and splashed into the river, soaking her hair half way up to her head.

"Aaahhhh," I breathed loudly, splashing some more water over my face. "Just like new." I stood up, with the water at my waist, then dipped my hair into the glacier melt and scrubbed it really hard. It felt good to get all the sweat off my body. I felt like a different man, not the rugged, dying mountain goat I was a day ago. My thick hair flopped down the side of my face, dripping into my eyes. She was right, the dark blue veins made it look like I had platinum poisoning, which was similar to what I really had. To a normal person, the boron nitride would be fatal within twenty-four hours. I don't think Walker even knew how this whole thing worked, but he knew what it was, and that it wouldn't kill me. He didn't know why I was different than everybody else. I was still a human, right? But after all this, I looked a little like the Bucromians, with the triangular markings on my wrist and the crystalized coating on my skin.

"My only remaining question for you, Jen, is how come your body reacted so heavily, and what caused it?" Tesla asked. I stopped as I was about to grab the white towel that hung on a sturdy bush, realizing I would have to tell her the truth.

"Walker gave me a fluid that gave me a hyper-realistic dream, which my body introduced as a vision, so it ended up with me being an emotional mess." I dried my hair thoroughly then wrapped the towel around my hips. "Your father was controlling you, I tried my best to get you back, but he was just in too deep." She gazed at the river, crossing her arms. "So I fought him out of wrath, and like every other time I try to protect someone I love, I got killed, with my own daggers, in front of you. And I heard you cry out to me, but I couldn't move, so I was left with my thoughts in excruciating pain till the world went blank," I finished. I grabbed the bleached blue jeans off the small bush, hopping up and down as I struggled to get them on.

"I understand what you mean, but it isn't the first time and it won't be the last. He will keep controlling me until you kill him, and you'll keep doing what you do best, protecting the world and nearly getting killed." Her words almost stopped my breathing. Did she believe I could protect the universe? If she did, that was enough to persuade me it was the right thing to do.

"You're sure I can stop this?" I tried to get my other leg in and almost fell over.

"Sure as heck," she answered confidently, flopping her hair back behind her head as soon as she was done ringing out the new braid. I slipped the cyan t-shirt over my head, then put my arms through the holes on the cool gray padded vest and grabbed my Erillia flashlight from my Cacadin suit and put it in my vest pocket. She gazed up at me with a surprised expression, taking in the new look as I struggled to balance while getting into my boa boots.

"Everything okay?" I paused to frown over at her as she wiped the expression off her face.

"It's been so long since I've seen you in normal clothes. It was starting to feel like Cacadin was your life," she contemplated. I was startled. I slowly walked over and grasped one of her hands in mine tightly as she continued to stare into the water.

"Maybe it is a good thing we got blown out of our spaceship then, eh?" I looked into her eyes, trying to understand her pain. "Cacadin wasn't my life, it's just . . . that was the only thing I was good at. But now, I have a purpose again, Tesla." She nodded, taking one more glance at the rushing water.

"You're right, how could I judge you when I've been doing exactly the same," she agreed, resting her head on my shoulder as I held her in a hug. "There's just been such a drastic change in both of us and we haven't really had the time to take it all in." She calmed her heavy breathing.

"I know, but we can fix this mess. We can still save Annoterra," *And my brother, wherever he is,* I thought bitterly.

I let go of her slowly and went back over to the small bush to retrieve my gear. Despite the freezing cold water, the heat was starting to come back fairly quickly. However, I was grateful to have some relief from the spiny pain. I headed back to camp behind Tesla, taking in the sunshine that filtered through the dense trees.

Aapi gave me a startled look as we entered the snowy clearing, her black eyes going up and down my torso.

"What? Outfit doesn't suit me?" I asked, missing the point as I glanced down at my clothes.

Hehe, you look fine! I just thought all you wore was dark, brooding wetsuits, Aapi joked.

Wetsuit? Aapi, it's a pioneer shell bodysuit, I corrected, folding up my Cacadin clothes and putting them in a pile.

The sooner I find my father and save my brother the better, less havoc for me, I resolved.

You have a brother? Aapi asked, shocked.

Forget you heard that. Can I ask you a favor? I sat down on the same log as before, poking the large rimmed fire with another stick I found. Tesla sat down beside me, leaning her lower back on the log, stretching her boots out towards the fire, and crossing her arms as comfortably possible.

Of course, Aapi affirmed.

If you can, don't intervene in my thoughts. I don't mean to be rude but…

No, I understand perfectly well. I'll try my best.

Thank you so much, Aapi.

"So, when should we leave?" Tesla interrupted the calm silence.

"Now," I decided quietly, heaving myself off the log. "If we stay here any longer we could get these Rebels killed. The sooner we find my father the sooner we can stop this war." Aapi stood up after me, snow dripping off her underbelly back onto the smooth imprint in the ground.

"You're gonna need this," Tesla remarked as she slapped my heavy gun holster into my hands.

"Why?"

"You tell me. If you can shoot a rock shelf with a sword, then by all means, leave it." I clipped the holster onto my belt reluctantly, tying it to my thigh.

"But can't I just turn my sword into a gun?" I asked.

"If you want to waste your resources," she replied. That made sense. A gun and a bullet can't be made from nothing. It would require an existing bullet, a mineral, or light source. She started to study her shifting map, peering at the new yellow line.

"What is that?" I pointed to the biggest dot connected to the line.

"The shards that the Rebels have collected to find Keaton. His known location hasn't been updated in the last few years, but it'll give us a chance," she said grimly, grabbing a small bag off another log.

"And that?"

"Food, water, computer viruses, first aid. I figured we better come prepared." She held up a small bismuth-like USB chip. I took it from her slowly and gazed into the geometric features, perplexed.

"What type of metal is this?" I didn't recognize it. The only thing I'd seen like it was a child's play sword with the same look, but this seemed real, like it had been taken right from the ground, not smelted or mixed with other metals.

"Regular Annoterra metal. It's like fool's gold, see the form?" She pointed to one of the square protrusions. "It's cubic."

"Huh." I handed it back to her as Aapi nudged me in the shoulder, urging me to stop wasting time.

"Well, I guess we better go then. I don't want to leave these people unprotected, but without my father we don't have any answers to the Bucromians' ancestry."

"They'll be fine," she giggled slightly as she heard the procrastination in my voice. She put her hand on my back and guided me into the bush, anxious to find answers.

CHAPTER 23

"Are you sure this is the right way?" I asked agitatedly after I sent a cascade of pebbles down the rigid ledge that opened into a wider pavilion-like area.

"I'm sure. Like I explained before, this map hasn't been updated in more than two years," Tesla replied.

I collapsed on the solid, snow-covered ground as she talked, trying to catch my breath as the higher elevation started to take over. The large snowflakes that tumbled from the sky distorted any view of the mountains, making the hike even more challenging. Aapi sat down beside my head, gazing at me impatiently.

"Now I'm the one slowing us down! What's wrong with me?" I panted as I sat up, trying to shake off the blurry vision that clouded my objective.

"Your body wasn't built for this elevation, it's normal," Tesla reassured me. She handed me the small canister out of the stiff black rucksack and I forced back a few gulps of the tasteless, mineral-rich water before putting the attached cap back on with shaky hands. I glared at the distant sun, its odd teardrop shape calming my breathing. It looked as if it was being sucked up effortlessly, burning the small planet behind it to a scorched off-black colour. The intimidating effect was the first thing that caught my eye in this man-made sector. Hyperion cloud had to be one of the most bizarre secrets still hidden from the eyes of society in our colonized galaxy.

Oh no . . . what have I done! Mother's probably grieving over my undead body! I stood up suddenly, then everything started to jump around in different shades of white. *No! Not again!* I abruptly dropped to the ground, blacked out from the lack of oxygen and blood to my brain.

"Jensen. Jensen! Wake up!" Tesla urged anxiously, shining the bright flashlight in my unresponsive eyes and smacking my jaw, setting everything back into motion unpleasantly. I sat up, my head throbbing with pressure built up like a soda can, trying to orientate myself as the world spun.

"Sit down, you giraffe," Tesla commanded playfully. I tried to stand up but she pushed me back down with all her weight, still shining the white light in my eyes.

"What happened?" she asked as I grabbed the flashlight from her and put it back in my pocket.

"As always, I tried to stand up and fainted," I answered irritatedly.

There were already enough challenges for me to push through in life. I didn't need my height getting in the way of saving an entire world, and possibly the entire galaxy. This had happened about a year ago, on my birthday, the one day I had off that year. The new non-gravity pools had just opened at Stratum Three, and Tesla, my mother and I had made plans to enjoy the many pools and hot tubs. So there I was, stepping out of one of the deep hot pools, when everything started to shift. I blacked out on the polished floor and was brought to the emergency room for a blood test. The doctor said I would be fine and just needed to heal up the gash I got on my forehead. My body was low on salt and water intake and had trouble keeping up with the low blood pressure caused by my height, so they suggested I get supplements to lessen the chance of it happening again. But of course, just like getting my eyes fixed from my nearsightedness, I refused and went about my daily life.

"Sounds logical," she shrugged, sitting down beside me. "Don't rush things, ok? I know it's been a long time since you've seen your father. But if he's out there, he can wait another minute or two."

"He's been gone twelve years, but that's not what I'm worried about." I lowered my vision to the rigid brown rock between my legs, which had been shuffled around.

"Your mother is fine, Jen. Just wait till you see her face when you go back to Earth with your father. She'll be relieved," Tesla reassured, grabbing the water bottle back out of the large pack.

I took a quick glance at Tesla as she drank from the clear cylinder bottle.

"Feeling better now?" she asked, standing up and hoisting the bag onto her back, putting her arms through the straps.

"I hope so. If not, I guess I should have accepted the supplements!" I joked, standing up slowly, making sure I didn't get light-headed again. She giggled quietly, trying to climb the slant onto the next level of rock. "You don't have anything to worry about. You're what, five foot nine?"

I asked as she managed to heave herself onto the next level, kicking a few cleaved shards of rock down towards us.

"Six feet, Jen," she snickered as I climbed up behind her, trying to find the vague foot holds.

"Shoot! One off!" I tried to catch my breath as I followed after her onto the snowy alpine.

"Uhh, Jensen, there are twelve inches in a foot," she laughed.

"Oh . . ." An embarrassed look spread across my face. "We'll say it was a Freudian slip," I paused. "Anyway, Aapi doesn't have to worry about this because she's, well, she's Aapi."

Aapi bounded off to the side in the powdery snow, sending clouds of fine icicles into the air. I'd never seen her have so much fun, leaping and crashing into the soft pillows that disguised small cedar-like trees as harmless lumps. Like a wild cat she pounced on a blanket of snow, then disappeared unexpectedly. I thought she had found a hidden creek bed, but her beak-shaped snout popped out of her fluffy covering and we all burst out laughing.

I live for this stuff! It's even better than water! she said excitedly.

It is water, it's frozen! Haha, you're talking to the geek of geeks! I tried to grab some snow and it melted as it hit my skin. She gawked at it in awe.

"Aw, man! That's all I want to do!" I shouted disappointedly as the water dribbled back onto the ground. "No more snowball fights for me."

That backfired horribly, Aapi sympathized. Her monotone thoughts broke off into a more appealing, hushed voice as she disappeared back into the pile. Tesla and I continued walking a little way before Aapi suddenly jumped out beside me and I staggered back into the snow, startled. The snow sizzled at my touch, making the sound effect even more comical than it should have been. Tesla let out a heartfelt cackle as Aapi picked me up off the snow apologetically.

"You should have seen your face! You were all like: Aaaa! Don't hurt me, mystical beast of the sea!" she teased as I let a toothy smile slide across my smooth oval face. We kept pacing along the steep cliff, keeping our distance from the treacherous tree-covered bowl across from us that looked like it could sluff down into the middle at any moment.

When I was little, I often watched the weather reports that showed the wide avalanches that came close to our house and scared Mother, most times almost persuading her that we should move. Our modern home would have been able to hold against an avalanche in the case of a large reaction. The valley we lived in near Sicamous wasn't exactly wide, so we had to take extra precautions. That's about all I could remember of my broken childhood on Earth.

"How far are we from my father's recent location?" I asked, slightly out of breath as I trudged through the deep snow.

"Another seven kilometers?" she answered, unsure, checking her map.

"So just over there?" I pointed to another cliff facing the one we were on, with a small, almost unnoticeable hangar. She nodded as I gazed at the weathered rock face, my heart rising in my throat at the mere thought. The stale memories of Father came back vividly. My father thought I was a bust.

He had said I was too tall for my age, that I had a temper, and that I was too smart for my own good. All I could hope for is that I could finally please him.

She patted my back before continuing the trek happily. I followed her through the set snow as we dropped back down in elevation, avoiding the steep drop off the pointed cliff. The two cliffs that faced each other looked as if they had once been a bridge. They were both pointed at the center into a long arrow shape, creating an entrance effect through the middle.

So, what was your father like from your perspective? I mean, to me he was the sweetest, most patient person I ever met, but if I were to expect emotions directed to his son . . . Aapi trailed off.

My father? He was cold. Either he envied my amazing piloting skills or he disapproved of my attitude and my reactions towards everything. He stole my childhood. He loved everyone but me.

She pulled up beside me, striding through the thick snow effortlessly with her webbed back feet on top of the snow like snowshoes, and her long pincer-like arms stretched out to find the right balance on the shifting ground.

That must have been hard. I wonder what happened. Her deep, sympathetic tone made it hard to hold back my tears, remembering the bitter life he gave me.

CHAPTER 24

Nordic J

I rested my chin on my knuckles, perplexed over the situation at hand.

"We really didn't think this through," Tesla said, kicking a rock across the ground below the hangar with the side of her foot.

"Nope. But I'm stubborn, so let's find a way in," I resolved. Stepping back from the overhang I stared up at the hangar. *Is that seriously the only way in? If it is, we're hooped.*

Being a good leader is to hide doubtfulness right? Well, that's what I'll do.

That's definitely not the right thing to do, Aapi glared at me sternly.

"Got any suggestions?" I asked after a few minutes. They both shook their heads. "Well, it doesn't help when there aren't any external wiring panels, unlike the combat droids I used to hack." Tesla gave me a you-did-what? look, screwing up her eyebrows with a mixture of I-didn't-know-you-knew-how-to-do-that and how-dare-you. I picked up a small piece of cleaved rock. "How would my father get out of his secret base that no one knows about?" I thought out loud, tapping my chin with the stone between my thumb and pointer. "What if part of the wall is a hologram?" I sighed, distrusting my judgment.

"I think I should go up and check it out," Tesla volunteered. She set the pack on the ground in a pile of flaking rock and quickly found footholds on the slick rock.

"What?" I jumped, watching as she climbed above my head.

"Maybe I can find out how to get in. Rock climbing was my specialty . . . with ropes." She reached her hand up to grasp another rock.

"You can't just put yourself out there and say, 'for the sake of Annoterra!'" I threw my arms up in the air fitfully. She growled irritatedly, muttering under her breath as she stretched her leg up to reach another piece of rock.

"Would you like to do it?" she asked impatiently, turning to stare at me. I opened my mouth to protest but decided she was right. She was the lightest. It was better than me or Aapi going up there. I was too tall, too broad. And Aapi couldn't go because . . . well, she was a crayfish, that's all there was to it. Also, Tesla said she'd trained for this, which should be all you need to win.

"Fine." I resigned. She continued to climb up the rock face, soon disappearing above the small, slippery overhang.

I sat down on a rock beside Aapi, twiddling my thumbs anxiously. Aapi turned her gaze towards me and tilted her head. I noticed what she was looking at and moved my wrist closer to her. I rested my cheek on my clenched fist, waiting for Tesla to pop out of the crag or something. Aapi calmly watched the colours shift, the luminous light bouncing around on the wall of rock in bright turquoise and greens.

I jumped slightly as I heard a loud metallic clicking sound coming from above my head, just below the overhang, about two hundred feet up. Part of the rock face slid up swiftly after a few seconds to reveal a low-lit interior, and out of that came Tesla's wide smile.

"That took way longer than expected! I had to hotwire one of the bulkheads because the coding was screwed," she admitted perkily, shrugging as she stepped out onto the edge of the platform.

"Wow, I never thought it was possible to move rock like that!" I was astonished, trying to find a foothold so I could heave myself up onto the pavilion. Aapi came up after me, panting slightly as she squeezed herself through the small corridor.

The air in the tight hall was fresh and smelled of clean rock and water, suggesting how long this had probably been here.

"Definitely still in use," I observed as I looked around at the shiny walls and floor. The tall ceiling had a few stalactites hanging from it here and there, and unlike the walls they were a rough, spongy stone.

My thoughts were cut off as a large drone came charging towards us. I extended my long sword into its chest, frying the circuits and sending brightly coloured sparks flying across the dark space.

Tesla suddenly shot past me, throwing herself at another drone and kicking it into the bulkhead on the other side.

My heart gave a horrible lurch as the room filled with vermilion red light, flashing on and off till my eyes screamed in agony.

"*Aapi!*" I yelled frustratedly at her frozen posture after she flung a droid out the door with her powerful tail, giving me her oops-I'm-busted expression. I didn't know how she had tripped the alarm till my eyes hit the broken stalactite on the floor beneath her large feet.

"You guys get out of here!" I urged, slashing a robot's head off.

"Why?" Tesla asked, pushing another off the small ledge with a clanging metal sound.

"It's too dangerous having more than one person in here! Just go, Axis!" I ordered, trying to unlock the bulkhead. She turned and rushed out of the hideout, Aapi hurrying behind her.

I swiftly sliced a robot through the torso before it could shoot me, pushing open the bulkhead with all my strength.

I hope that's the last one! I thought as I moved through the heavy steel door and closed it behind me. The air inside was warmer and smelled of smoke and cut grass. The only things lighting the wide hall were my marks and a small LED lamp that filled the passageway with a dim, warm glow.

Up or forward? Bulkhead or ladder? I asked myself as I gazed up the shaft into the dark area above, then over at the coded bulkhead across from me. I gave a small shrug and headed up the ladder, my blue impressions flooding the small area.

I sure hope Father is here. I saw a dull, almost unnoticeable light at the top of the passage, giving me hope. I stepped into a pitch black area, squinting around the room as best I could. I discovered where the light was coming from and picked it up off the small table, gazing into the bright picture, illuminated by its glowing clear frame.

In the picture were Tesla, Nixon, Kaizer, and my father, sitting cheerfully in front of the scenic mountain range. They all looked so young, with their unblemished faces and wide smiles. Tesla's hair was short, only reaching her collarbone. I'm sure it must have been a tad longer though, because it was tied up in neat little braids.

I never imagined her any different than what I've been used to. Why was she here? From what she told me, she was born on Earth. Our entire lives are a lie . . .

I set the picture back on the table and peered around a little more, noticing the coffee machine and tall fridge that sat by a long counter. I moved around the island towards another ladder, hoisting myself up the vertical steps. My glowing wrist served as a helpful tool, lighting the dark so I could inspect the tidy rooms.

The area above the kitchen looked as if it was gear storage, filled with sealed helmets and suits, chest plates, boots, an assortment of gloves, transmitters, beacons, probes, avalanche packs, bodysuits, ski pants, and jackets.

I've never seen so much gear in one place! It's a pioneer's heaven. Maybe Father would let me take a beacon later, I thought as I inspected one of the small phone-like devices hanging by their straps on the wall. In the far corner I found the bulkhead that had been screwed off its hinges by my girlfriend and was now lying on the floor. I stepped over the thick metal into the hangar, where I found a white hover bike sitting elegantly.

"Whoa," I chuckled as I ran my hand along one of the hovering cylinder plates. *Enough kicking tires, Jen! Time to find Father!* I urged myself, heading back out of the hangar towards the next ladder. I started to climb when suddenly something kicked me back down and I thumped onto the glossy floor, the air pushed out of my chest. He landed on top of me, his thin sword up against my neck. For a long moment, time seemed to stop as I glared into the lens that covered the attacker's eyes and cheeks. I took in all his features, the square shoulders, long arms, skinny torso, stout chin, straight nose.

But something was odd. If this was my father, why did he look like he was in his late thirties? Why was he still in such good shape?

He dropped his weapon beside my head, the loud clanging sound sending a sharp pain through my skull. He staggered back in shock, and as soon as he let go of me I crawled backwards till my back hit the wall. He tapped a small button under his jaw and the lens disappeared into the small slate. I stared into my father's deep blue eyes as he teared up. My words caught in my throat every time I tried to say his name.

EPILOGUE

The following is a preserved memory...

Two familiar voices from the pavilion above snapped me out of the action in my book. I quickly slapped the yellow hardcover down on the padded chair and jogged over to the large steps.

"What do you expect me to do, Nixon? I can't make the same mistake as my kind did on Earth. We can't have a government, so what do we do? At this point I'm all ears to your adapted mind," Father said, his low voice betraying his irritation.

"We could just let the public eye be the government, and we could make the final decision," I heard Nixon's smooth voice, a little farther away, supposedly by the window. "At least then they get a say in things."

"First, we would have to persuade them that constructive debate and criticism is the way to go," Father reasoned.

I walked up the steps to see their perplexed faces as they gazed over at me. "Hello, Nixon," I waved politely to his small smile. "Father, you wouldn't happen to know where Tesla is, would you?" Disinterested in my question, he turned back to the holographic plan table. "I mean, I've looked all over, the courtyard, her room, even the aquifer." I rubbed the back of my stiff neck.

"Kaizer . . ." Father began impatiently.

"I mean, even I thought she would be there! Man, she must be really good at hide—" I tried to continue.

"Kaizer!" he cut through my rambling with his stern voice. Nixon gave him a just-tell-the-truth look, and he let out a disturbed sigh. "Tesla's gone, don't ask me where," he said.

"Can I ask Nixon?" I asked, gazing over at the tall Bucromian expectantly. Tesla was my only friend. Even though she was about four years younger than me, she was almost as smart and was definitely more cautious when talking to someone.

As far as I understood from the many fragments of conversations I had overheard, Tesla's mother didn't actually give birth to her, the genetics were simply mixed and BOOM! There she was, just like Aapi. *Fabricated.*

"No, you—" Father began.

"She went back to Earth to watch over your brother," Nixon said briskly, crossing his arms.

"Nixon!" my father shouted, just outside of his inside voice.

"Why? That was the last place she wanted to be!" I hollered as tears filled my pale green eyes.

"Let's put it this way. Here, I'll show you." Father picked me up so I could see the large platform. He pulled up a large picture of a DNA strand. "See this, Kaizer? This is your brother's DNA. But you see that little piece over there?" He pointed to a slightly different, blue-coloured section.

"Yes, what is it?" I asked. He zoomed in on it and pulled up the picture so it was a hologram floating in the scent-less air.

"We're not sure. But your brother's life is in danger. There are corrupt people out in our galaxy, looking for . . . umm . . . super naturals like your brother. When they find him, they will use him against his will as a weapon." He pulled the picture of the small settlement up again, setting me back down.

"What type of weapon? Like a conductive material, or a monster?" I asked worriedly.

"We're not sure. Hopefully conductive." Even though he said the word hopefully, his eyes were still clouded with worry and pain.

"So, Tesla is protecting my brother so the galaxy doesn't die? So that he can live a full, undisturbed life?"

"Yes. I'm surprised you figured it out that quickly," he gaped at me with an astonished glint in his eyes. "How did you figure it out?" he asked.

"Well, I read a lot of war-type books . . . and I've kind of seen it in certain people on Earth. They've walked past me or whatever and given me a destructive glare. Or it's their tone. I heard it in one of the Cacadin agents. I think he was just having a bad day," I shrugged, and looked out the window to see an Avigull crash into the clear glass. The men exchanged confused glances as I spewed out information as I always did. "May I go play with Aapi now? I think she would appreciate that Avigull that just ran into the window. I'd be sad, but it was really funny," I giggled as I tried to spot the bird from the window.

"Of course, go ahead," my father answered breathlessly. I headed out the door, racing down the stairs and throwing on my thick gray sweater as I jogged past my chair.

2133pioneer

My father had created the code as that specific date because that was the year he created Annoterra. It was the most exciting year of his life. Even though I hadn't been born yet, I have read all his journal entries and books.

I punched in the numbers quickly to unlock the door, letting in a gust of cold air. I stepped out, then made sure the door had closed all the way behind me.

"Hey, Aapi! Want an Avigull?" I asked, gesturing to the dead bird on the ground, its feathers swaying with the wind. She gazed up at me happily as she buried herself in the snow. She stood up after a few seconds and ran over towards the bird.

"Awww, what happened to it?" she asked, poking it with one of her pincers.

"It hit the window," I stated nonchalantly. I pointed to the office window about two hundred feet up.

"Ah, I see. It looked pretty silly, too, didn't it?" She grabbed the Avigull and started to rip through it.

"Yeah," I rubbed my book-worm neck again. "Gosh, I still can't believe she's gone," I said.

Aapi gazed up at me curiously. "Who?" she asked, finishing off the bird and tossing it off the cliff.

"Tesla." I answered gloomily.

"But, isn't it good that your brother will be safe? I'm sure she'll come back to us someday, Kaizer."

I snapped back into reality as soon as I felt the zephyr break below my ship and I entered the crusty atmosphere, pulling back my steering so I could slow down. I navigated my small ship between rock faces to land in a narrow space, hidden from any watching eyes.

This is such a bad idea. But how else am I going to stop Nixon? Now or never, the Rebels are failing to do their job. I unbuckled myself from the comfy bucket seat and pulled a small lever to retract it into the empty position. I walked towards the door, opened a small compartment, and heaved out a heavy bag, which I opened to grab a snocross helmet.

Hue should be fine, right? I'll only be gone an hour or two. I set my helmet on gently as I peered over at the dark purple, six-legged dragon on the dog bed, his back heaving up and down slowly. *He'll be fine,* I reassured myself as I buckled the strap on my helmet and secured the polarized goggles on my face in the most comfortable position. The cab immediately filled with hot air as I swung open the door. I looked down quickly to find the cliff edge, seeing barely enough space for me to hop out. I adjusted the straps on my neon green monosuit, then jumped out of the white ship onto the hot surface. I closed the hatch with a slam and hesitated as I looked over the small ledge.

Is this really the right thing to do? I second guessed myself as I shuffled my helmet on its neck brace and continued to stare down the sharp cliff to the sparse trees below. I put my hands through the arm holes and zipped up my heat-repelling monosuit, finished tying up my X-Cross boots, then adjusted my clothes further as I took in the view. I stepped back as far as I could from the crag and ran forward off it, putting my arms through two straps on my suit and pulling open a thick webbing-like material. I gazed down at the ground as it got farther away, taking in the new scenery and gliding on the drafts of air that sent me up higher every time, then down slightly into a faster dive. The sparse dragonblood trees spread across the horizon like a wall of fire, dotting it with shades of green and pink as the sun rose. The lanky cactus below me cast long shadows, giving the various small animals shelter till the sun rose entirely to its unforgiving heat. I dropped down to the ground slowly, popping a spring-loaded dial to eject an airfoil, pulling to a stop on the sand.

My stealthy approach didn't go unnoticed. Far off I heard numerous rumbles, coming closer by the minute till I saw the speckled horizon. The smallest of the ships landed about twenty feet in front of me, turning its engines off as soon as it touched the sandy ground. The gate lowered, exposing the hydraulic jacks as the ramp descended. I unbuckled my helmet and attached it to the small clips on the shoulder blades of my suit.

"I warned you not to come back here, Galantis." A wealthily dressed Acolite strode down the ramp. I chuckled slightly as I peered at his tall, slender figure.

"Well, isn't that sw—"

"Skedaddle, before I kill you," he ordered as he suddenly came nose-to-nose with me, giving me a cold stare.

"Hear me out. You could make a lo—" I tried to reassure him.

"I don't want any part of that—" he began.

I cut him off by pulling my gun out of the holster and shooting one of the war cruisers out of the sky. It hit the ground in a cloud of flames and web-like electrical waves. He backed off slightly, giving me room to speak.

"I can't seem to get a word in edgewise with you people! Hear me out," I urged again. The tall, pale orange Acolite narrowed his eyes at me in disgust. "The war is spreading, Nixon's technology and telepathic abilities are evolving, so to speak. If you help me, you can have all the Bucromians you want for your arena of misery," I bargained. I put my gun back in its sleek burgundy holster as he tapped his chin, lowering his gaze to the ground as if to look enlightened, but still trying to make a decision with his undivided attention.

"Hmm . . . I suppose that's fair. What do you want in return?" he asked worriedly, as if I would try to take over Cayyam, the planet richest in every type of mineral imaginable. That wasn't my motive. All of the watching eyes turned towards me as I opened my mouth to answer with a toothy smile:

"The most powerful weapon in the universe."

ABOUT THE AUTHOR

Leilani Frantik is a young Canadian writer. Leilani's love for writing began shortly before her twelfth birthday, when she travelled with her family to Sicamous, B.C., to enjoy balmy winter days. The wintery, mountainous landscape inspired Leilani to write her first book, Renegade, which is the first in a series titled "Blizzardia." The character Jensen nearly took on a life of his own and presented a compelling story. After several rough drafts and months of funnelling creative energy, Renegade emerged completed, to Leilani's delight. When she is not writing, Leilani enjoys spending time in the mountains with her family, doing activities such as snowmobiling, camping, watching wildlife, and being out in the woods. She currently lives in Unity, Saskatchewan, with her parents and younger brother. The family also has a dry cabin in Leoville, Saskatchewan, and continue to visit Sicamous whenever they can.

✦—○—✦

THE UNLIKELY CANDIDATES

✦—○—✦